THE
Good Book

THE
Good Book
A Case For Following Jesus Christ

Some Keys

to Finding Happiness and Truth in Your Life

MELVIN DOUGLAS WILSON

TATE PUBLISHING
AND ENTERPRISES, LLC

Published by Tate Publishing & Enterprises, LLC
127 E. Trade Center Terrace | Mustang, Oklahoma 73064 USA
1.888.361.9473 | www.tatepublishing.com

Tate Publishing is committed to excellence in the publishing industry. The company reflects the philosophy established by the founders, based on Psalm 68:11,
"The Lord gave the word and great was the company of those who published it."

Book design copyright © 2014 by Tate Publishing, LLC. All rights reserved.
Cover design by Junriel Boquecosa
Interior design by Joana Quilantang

Published in the United States of America

ISBN: 978-1-62902-892-7
1. Fiction / Christian / Classic & Allegory
2. Religion / Christian Life / Inspirational
13.11.14

Dedication

This book is dedicated to my mother, who believed immensely in me, and also to my father, who thought that I would not amount to much. What we clearly see in the above statement is that sometimes in life, it takes both extremes to be part of a molding process for God to produce his final product.

Acknowledgments

I first would like to thank the Lord Jesus Christ for all of the wisdom, knowledge, and understanding that is spelled out in this book, and it is my prayer that people will seek positive changes in their lives.

I would also like to thank my wife, who has been my lover, my friend, and my soul mate. My wife is the answer to my many prayers and a true gift from God.

Disclaimer

The characters in this book are real people in most cases; however, they are sometimes based on true life experiences. Also, the people in all of the parables are in no way any type of secret knowledge, but based on strong Bible doctrine that can be found in your King James Bible.

The Goal
of this Book

This book was not written to become the light in your life, but to point you to the truth and the true light, which is Jesus Christ. The goal of this book is for you to find Jesus Christ in your life or to strengthen an existing relationship with him after reading this book.

Contents

Foreword

The turbulent winds of change are blowing across this great nation of ours and not necessarily for the good of this nation or for the good of mankind in general. These winds of change must be calmed by a national revival of change concerning the declining moral state of this country and the world today. If we as a nation do not change, I am afraid that history may repeat itself and this great, rich, and prosperous nation of ours may end up like the late great Roman Empire. We must acknowledge that the Roman Empire was not destroyed by invading armies in the beginning, but was destroyed by the declining moral behavior of the people within the empire.

In our society today, we do not use the slogans or words that used to be honorable anymore. Such as brotherly love, honesty, modesty, hospitality, or integrity. You see that what we once thought of at one time in this country's history as positive has now become negative. People in this country are now simply seeking to do evil, and disguising the evil as something good so that they can tolerate their sinful behavior. I will give you a few examples.

It is all right if you shoot heroin into your veins, rob your momma and everyone else in sight, but please make sure them dirty heroin addicts have clean needles to use. It is also all right for the youth in this country to go out to nightclubs, get sloppy drunk, and waste all of their time and money on the weekends at these filthy nightclubs, but please make sure that you find them a designated driver. Again, it is all right for us married folks to have extramarital sex, but please put on a clean condom when committing a very dirty act, such as infidelity. Whatever happened to the truth in this country, and why do we now tolerate sinful behavior?

This book is about dramatic change for your life and some suggestions on how to stop these problems that we are facing in this country. This country has gone through dramatic change before, but never like what are experiencing today.

The superficial look is now being courted by all age groups and all cultures in our society today. In the African-American community alone, hair care products (weaves/fake hair), nails, and pedicures are now a multi-billion-dollar business. Americans are spending billions of dollars to perform surgery on everything from breast enlargements, tummy tucks, rear-end enhancements (butt lifts), face-lifts, and everything else people can think of to enhance the outer you in society today.

The only problem with all of these procedures and lifts is that nothing is being done to address the real problem in most cases, which is the inner you. The root cause for all of these problems is a lack of happiness and a lack of hope in people's lives.

In this book, we will see that this unhappiness comes into a person's life based on trying to become happy outside of having a true relationship with God.

This is why, once you start with these procedures to attain your happiness outside of a relationship with God, this happiness is only short lived. Then you will only try to duplicate another procedure to keep this perception of happiness alive in your mind. Recently, an aging movie actress said in a press conference, "I am spending a lot of money on plastic surgery to look so cheap."

Whatever happened to the time in this country when people worked at being happy based on the Holy Scriptures and the absolute truth in the Word of God? Why did we go down this slippery slope and start believing that the virtues that we lived by in yesteryears have no place in this postmodern society that we now live in?

I submit to you, my brothers and sisters, that we must go back to the old ways of thinking, where inner beauty is appreciated and modesty is applauded in a woman instead of the amount of cleavage that she might be showing. We are now living in a time where we are currently seeing women coming to church with their breasts hanging out, exposed for all to see, and these women somehow think that they look good. God forbid.

This book is not going to help you to become a good person, but is a starting point for your transformation. You will have to seek the Word of God to truly be a good person. Our main problem in this nation is that we do not want to hear the truth in most cases, so we will then just keep stumbling through life trying to get things right under our own power.

We are now seeing numerous attacks on the Word of God by a society that just wants to have it their way, and it is hard to know what is right or wrong. This is why mankind must have only one written authority to govern our lives, which is the Holy Bible.

In the Old Testament Book of Judges, we see that in the history of the nation of Israel, during a time when there was no consistent leadership in that nation, "every man did that which was right in his own eyes." We are currently at this point now, in this country where we are teaching tolerance instead of the Word of God in the correct context. We are now seeing most churches spending Sunday after Sunday entertaining the congregation, and no one is getting saved or being helped to become a better person. This book is about positive change that can only occur where the true Word of God is being preached and people are truly seeking God. My suggestion to all my brothers and sisters is to read this book, find a strong Bible-believing church, and then start seeking God for positive change in your life immediately.

The characteristics of someone who is seeking God are listed below. Do you fit one or more of these characteristics?

1. A seeker is a person who is not overly religious because the road to hell is paved with overly religious people standing in line, waiting to get in.

2. A seeker does not seek religion, but a true and lasting relationship with our Lord and Savior Jesus Christ.

3. A seeker is a person who achieves constantly by the power of God and whose lifestyle is a testimony of the faith that he or she has in God. This faith can be clearly seen.

It is the heart of a person and the power of God operating in us that determines our net worth in this society we now live in and not the amount of worldly, witty thinking or conspicuous consumption that he or she might attain here on this earth. We, as Americans, must spend more time and effort developing godly character and putting love into our spirits, so that this love will be manifested in us. Then we can start sharing this love with others.

Summary

In the world today, we have many multibillion-dollar businesses to make people look better outside, but only God can make you look better inside. We must understand that these flesh and bone bodies will one day pass away, but our relationship with Jesus Christ will determine where we will spend eternity and what reward we will receive in glory. My dear brothers and sisters, you do not need a plastic surgeon to approach God, but only to believe in his son, Jesus Christ, who is the mediator between God and all mankind. Please be blessed reading this book and finding Jesus Christ in your life. This is my prayer for the world.

Amen.

Reality

Seeking the Truth

And ye shall know the truth, and truth shall make you free.

John 8:32 (KJV)

As we start on this long journey together to seek the truth in our lives, we must understand that this book deals with an accepted reality that this author and millions of other people share. This reality is that the Bible is the final authority of man, and that Jesus Christ is our Lord and Savior. This book is by no means intended to become your Bible, but it is intended to point you toward the Holy Bible and to find a meaningful relationship with Jesus Christ.

The first word that we will look at in this book will be the word *reality*. This word is important because without a true sense of reality in your life, you will never find the truth. People who have not found reality in their lives seem to create their own sense of reality, and most of the time, this reality does not conform to the reality of others. This issue concerning reality reminds me of a friend of mine named Randy. Randy could never find a lasting relationship with any of the girls that he dated due to his inability to find that perfect girl that was embedded deep down inside of Randy's mind. If a girl that he dated was not that perfect picture of what Randy had pictured in his mind, Randy was not interested. Poor Randy would try Internet dating and all kinds of other methods, trying to find this perfect woman, but every time, these dates would never work out and the relationship would end abruptly. The problem with Randy is that he had created his own sense of reality of what the perfect woman would be like in his mind, but this perfect woman in Randy's mind is not real, and she does not truly exist.

My dear friend Randy is like millions of people in the world today who are now wandering around aimlessly without a true sense of reality or an absolute truth working in their lives. These people can only depend on their own sense of reality, which is only based upon how they perceive the world. The main drawback with self-perception in people is that people who depend on self-perception are usually only trying to please themselves and will never find true happiness with other people.

To further complicate matters even more, finding reality in our lives today is now becoming an American obsession in this country. People in this postmodern society are now binding together to form cliques to pool their own ideas of what is right and what is wrong. The rich have one idea of what the truth should be, and the poor have another idea of what they think the truth should be.

The Republican Party in this country has their own sense of reality as does the Democratic Party, which has now created gridlock and a non-compromising tone in this nation's political system. In the inner cities, gangs have created their own sense of reality based on their environment and a warped sense of the truth, which is now getting a lot of young black men, who trust in the reality that these groups bring to them, killed every day.

The TV industry has created what they call reality television, but no one is finding love on these television shows or projecting a true sense of reality. Please tell the truth, has anyone ever found love after hosting numerous television shows looking for love? The answer is no. When will the world find out that they cannot find love or the truth outside of having a loving relationship with Jesus Christ?

My dear brothers and sisters, we cannot live in a society where the truth as we know it is a moving target with changing values that do not safeguard our homes or our nation. I solicit that you find the truth in God's Word, and he will set your feet on the right path to finding a true purpose for your life.

The Holy Bible was given to mankind for God's divine purpose of establishing the truth, and without the Word of God present, you will become lost trying to establish your own truth and reality in an evil world. We will discuss this issue concerning reality and the truth in more detail throughout this book, so be ready.

Now I wish to discuss another important issue that is plaguing America today, which is the rise of evil in this country and the decline of true moral behavior. This subject is very important in the wake of all of the violence that is now gripping this country.

The Parable of the Spirit that Whispers, which you will read about later, has many theological doctrines that you may, or may not, be able to understand. So I am using the favorite teaching method of Jesus Christ to paint a vivid picture of the truth in your mind. It is my hope that you discover a true sense of reality in your life and will understand that this world has evil forces keeping you from the truth.

Remember that most people in this country believe that there is a Christian God of this universe, based on every recent poll taken. The problem is that in these same polls, most people do not believe in the devil or the presence of evil in this world. I hope that after you read the Parable of the Spirit that Whispers that you will believe that evil does truly exists, and people should understand that the devil and the forces of evil are a part of our earthly reality. I would love to just focus on the good in the world, but if you are not aware of evil in the world, you can be severely hurt when evil rears its ugly head in your life. We will continue to educate ourselves throughout this book on the forces of evil working against us.

Before you read the Parable of the Spirit that Whispers, you will need to have a general understanding on how parables work and the main purpose for writing parables. This book will contain other parables, and you must understand this author's vision is based on the Holy Scriptures to help to paint a vivid picture of these stories in your mind.

The word *parable* is derived from a Greek word meaning "signifying or to compare together." A parable is a short allegorical story designed to illustrate or teach some truth, religious principle, or moral lesson.

Source:http://dictionary.reference.com/browse/ parable

The objective of a parable is:

To see it in your mind and ask: How can I apply this truth to life? We must use our mind and see this parable being acted out.

Please enjoy the Parable of the Spirit that Whispers and remember to read this parable with your mind.

The Parable of the Spirit that Whispers

THE REALITY OF EVIL

In the beginning of time, in a far and distant land, there was a king called Americus. He was a very loving king and very protective to all of his loyal subjects. Americus the King also recognized the spiritual needs of his people. The king worshipped and loved the Good Spirit and was a very righteous and upright man. The king would build great worship centers for the people to openly praise and worship the Good Spirit. This true praise and worship of the Good Spirit kept the balance of evil in his kingdom in check, and during the reign of King Americus evil never flourished in his kingdom.

During the reign of Americus, the Good Spirit gave the king the ability to discern the Spirit that Whispers. Americus would then train his people to resist the evil spirit and to seek to do good. Americus knew that by identifying this spirit as evil the people would not be tricked into accepting this evil spirit into their homes or into their hearts and minds. Americus knew the tricks of this evil spirit by reading the Books of Old.

The Books of Old told the stories of the Spirit that Whispers and how this particular spirit was only bent on one thing: death and destruction to anyone whom he came in contact with. Americus also knew that, based upon the Books of Old, the Spirit that Whispers is doomed to the lake of fire and now wants to take as many people with him as possible.

During the reign of Americus, the Good Spirit was loved and praised, and this love spread to all of the people in the kingdom. The people in the kingdom also loved each other immensely, and the kingdom flourished, but after many years of loving kindness to his people and total dedication to the Good Spirit, the king would now be taken home to be with the Good Spirit for eternity.

Americus's son, Europa, would now be crowned king and continue in the ways of his father. Europa, like his father, kept open the worship centers and also embraced the Good Spirit. The only thing that Europa did different from his father was to ignore the Spirit that Whispers, and Europa would not read the Books of Old. He would tell his loyal subjects that the Spirit that Whispers was just a fairy tale, a myth, and not to be concerned about this weak spirit. During the reign of Europa, the Good Spirit continued to be known and loved by only the older people of his kingdom, but something was keeping the younger generation of people away from the Good Spirit. So now the Good Spirit would start sending out his prophets to warn the people about their sinful ways and their evil lifestyles, but this new generation of people were not listening.

Soon, Europa would die and his son, Asiaia, would now become king. Asiaia continued in the ways of his father and kept open the worship centers, but Asiaia did not truly believe in the Good Spirit. By now, all of the original elders were gone, and the worship of the Good Spirit was performed by just about anyone and not the appointed priest based on the Books of Old.

A new group of people were spreading dissention and sin across the kingdom, and no one knew whom these people were linked to. It was like a new generation of evil people was changing the lifestyles of the good people of the kingdom without an established leader.

The new theme of the people was "to do what feels good" and "to do it my way" with no consideration for the other people of the kingdom. This new group of wicked people spread like wildfire, and before long, the whole kingdom was in turmoil.

The king now ordered an immediate investigation on what was causing the people in his kingdom to be so sinful, but all of his wise men could not give him an answer. The king soon inquired to the temple fathers, but they also could not give him a straight answer. The now frustrated king wrote out a proclamation, telling the people that anyone who could stop this tide of sinful behavior would be rich, but again, the people could not give him a good answer.

Evil continued to spread in the kingdom at an alarming rate. The kingdom where everyone loved each other was now gone. At this point, the king would give up and shut himself up inside of his castle and wait for these evil people to overrun his kingdom.

Now, while the king had become a virtual prisoner in his own castle, he started reading the Books of Old to pass the time and came across the chapters concerning the Spirit that Whispers. The king soon found out as he read the books that all of the problems that were going on in his kingdom were all characteristics of this evil Spirit that Whispers. The king shouted aloud when it finally came to his mind that the Spirit that Whispers was disclaimed as a myth or a fairy tale by the past kings. Asiaia continued to read the Books of Old, and he found out that the Spirit that Whispers was named the devil, satan, and lucifer and that his greatest trick on mankind is to make people think that he does not exist. The king glanced further into the books and read that if people do not believe that the Spirit that Whispers truly exists, there is no defense against his schemes and methodology.

The king had now discovered the truth, but his kingdom was still doomed because nobody would believe him. All of the people who believed in the Good Spirit were now dead or taken to other kingdoms where the Good Spirit was flourishing. Soon, evil overran the once peaceful, loving, and tranquil kingdom, and the king was pulled from his castle fortress and killed. In his last statement, he warned the people to watch out for the Spirit that Whispers, but it was too late. The evil people, now the majority in his kingdom, just shook their heads, saying aloud that he is now trying to blame all of his problems on a myth or a fairy tale. Asiaia would die and wake up in hell, and he would now spend eternity with the Spirit that Whispers.

In hell, the king, while being tormented, wished that he would have read the Books of Old sooner, but now he only has the memories of his lost opportunities that will haunt him forever both day and night 24/7.

Chapter One Summary

In the world today, mankind needs to have a sense of reality that is in concert with the people around you. If you do not have a sense of what is real, you will just create reality for yourself or with others. This plan is sending people to a very bad place called hell.

I submit to you that the Holy Bible is the final authority for man. This way, man has one set of rules to live by, and mankind can now follow an established pattern in life.

Mankind needs to be aware of the forces of evil working in this world today. Most people believe in heaven, but do not believe in evil or that hell truly exists.

The greatest trick the devil has played on mankind is to have mankind believe that the devil does not exist. *The devil is real.*

Summary of the Spirit that Whispers

The moral of the Spirit that Whispers is that we must recognize that the devil is not a figment of a Christian's imagination. The devil is real and should be avoided, shunned, and resisted by standing firm in our faith in God.

The church must keep training and equipping future leaders with the tools to succeed, or the next generation of leaders can easily be lost. Pray for the leadership of this country and the leadership at your local church.

This lesson on leadership is given to us in the Old Testament in the Books of Kings.

Your memory never dies in hell. This will be another form of torment.

Scripture Memorization: 1 Peter 5:8–9

> Be sober, be vigilant; because your adversary the devil, as a roaring lion, walketh about, seeking whom he may devour. Whom resist stedfast in the faith, knowing that the same afflictions are accomplished in your brethren that are in the world.
>
> 1 Peter 5:8–9 (KJV)

Religion/Relationship

The Art of Playing Church

> Thou believest that there is one God; thou doest
> well: the devils also believe, and tremble.

James 2:19 (KJV)

In the world today, there are many religions to choose
from, with all of these religions claiming that they are
representing the true God of the universe. It is my prayer
that you find the truth and establish a lasting relationship
with Jesus Christ.

Now let us try to understand the truth about the
word *religion*. This word *religion* must be understood correctly,
so that you will never become a religious person.
In most churches today, the vast majority of the people
that attend are considered religious people. I know that
you have heard the slogan, "That Melvin is a very religious
man," but what this terminology really means is
that Melvin goes through the rituals of Church.

Let us now look at the definition of the word *religion*:

"A religion is a set of common beliefs and practices generally held by a group of people, often codified as prayer, ritual, and religious law. Religion also encompasses ancestral or cultural traditions, writings, history, and mythology, as well as personal faith and mystic experience. The term "religion" refers to both the personal practices related to communal faith and to group rituals and communication stemming from shared conviction."

Source: http://www.moonlightchest.com/
religion/default.asp

As we see in this definition of the word *religion*, it says little to nothing about a personal relationship with Jesus Christ. The definition of the word *religion* means that you may practice a set of common beliefs with other people, but what if these other people that you practice your set of beliefs are on their way to a burning hell? Would you then want to follow these people to hell for eternity?

There are many people in today's churches just going through the motions Sunday after Sunday, some saved by the grace of God and some not. Throughout this entire book, the goals will always remain the same, which is to have a meaningful relationship with Jesus Christ at all cost. I have joined only two churches in my Christian life and I have met some truly good Christian people, and I have also met some truly bad Christian people. But as I sit here writing this part of the book, I can never say that the Lord has ever let me down. I have let him down the majority of the time.

In this chapter, we can see clearly that the word *religious* is not the goal of a Christian brother or sister. Again, we must seek a lasting relationship with God.

THE ART OF PLAYING CHURCH

A great man once said that between the hours of eleven o'clock Sunday morning and two o'clock Sunday afternoon is the most segregated time of the week for most Americans. What this great man meant was that black Americans go to their own churches in most cases, and white Americans go to their own churches in most cases. Today, things have changed somewhat, based on the New Evangelical multicultural churches, but during these hours on Sunday, millions of people are out worshipping God in their collective churches.

I will call this entire group of people attending church on Sunday Christendom. But within this overall group in Christendom, there is another group of people who are professional churchgoers who go to church every Sunday with no change from their worldly concepts or no real happiness showing in their lives.

My definition of a professional churchgoer is a person or a family of people who go to church every Sunday and know how to talk, walk, and act like Christians until Monday morning rolls around, and then they somehow revert back to their worldly selves. Some of these professional churchgoers will even revert back to their worldly selves right out in the church parking lot, so be very careful when addressing these people. It can get very ugly!

Now we are going to take the time to examine another three subgroups of people that make up most local church congregations. Please remember in chapter 1, we discussed the presence of evil in the world. Evil is alive and well in the world and also in most churches.

The first group of people who are just waiting for you at some local churches is the devil's people. This first group of people at your local church will seek you out, but they will now be easy for you to spot because of this warning listed below, so beware.

The devil's people will be a person, a family, or a group of people that will walk up to you and continue to ask you all kinds of personal questions, probing to find some type of weakness in your character to exploit. Just be as polite as possible and stay away from these people. You see, the devil and his people are very religious people and are very well connected in most churches. Remember, the search for the truth both begins and ends with your eyes fixated on Jesus Christ and not man.

The first goal for the forces of evil once that they have found a new God-loving Christian in a local church is to destroy their sense of purpose in that church and in the world for Jesus Christ. You see, once your sense of purpose has been destroyed and your integrity is stripped from you, then you are no longer a threat to the devil's people. You then become just another religious person that cannot be used by God, if you do not change your ways and confess your sinful behavior to the Lord.

The second goal of the devil's people is to try to disconnect you from an unlimited power source that works in a true believer's heart, which is the Holy Spirit. If they can accomplish this goal, then you become a professional churchgoer as described above with no love, no happiness, or no power of God working in your life.

The second group of people that you will come in contact with in some local churches is a group that worships men. I call them the pastor's people. The pastor's people will never have the power of God working in their lives because they are at church for only one reason: to impress the Pastor, instead of the Master of the universe. Anytime that you honor men, you are just looking for trouble because man will always let you down sooner or later.

I have seen many people get terribly hurt in some churches and will never darken the doors of the church again after being hurt by an evil pastor. Please love your pastor and pray for your pastor, but put your trust and your heart in God's hands only. This will keep you from getting hurt in the curiosity stage of Christian development.

This book is to help you to have a meaningful relationship with Jesus Christ and to warn you of the pitfalls along the way. The keys to life will not change in this book from cover to cover. To keep the main thing, which is Jesus Christ, in your life first, and never change this process.

The third and last group of people that make up the local church is the Lord's people.

These people, who are at all of the local churches, will be a little bit harder to find at first because the Lord's people are not looking for you at all. The Lord's people do not try to impress man or work for the devil. The Lord's people sole reason for being in the church is to glorify God. These are the people that you are looking for to fellowship with once you make the correct choice to follow God.

These are the people who will take you under their wings and nurture you, helping you to grow in power and in strength. These are the people who will earnestly pray for you and not prey on you and truly will protect you. Please find the Lord's people when you make your mind up to follow Jesus Christ and at all cost be obedient to them. The Lord's people will help you get through the tough times and will be a vital ally in spotting the devil's team at your local church.

Church Leadership

My dear brothers and sisters, we are experiencing some real dark days in church leadership today. The morality of the leadership structure of most churches is sinking. It seems like every time you pick up the newspaper, you are reading about another church scandal. On the evening news last night, the Catholic Church has just settled a hundred million dollar child abuse case in California, and in Connecticut, a storefront preacher was convicted of fathering a child by a thirteen-year-old girl in his congregation.

We are not only seeing the moral decline in most churches, but we are also seeing the lust for money rearing its ugly head in most churches. In many of the churches across this country, we are seeing some flamboyant pastors driving expensive automobiles, while the people in their congregation struggle to pay their bills. The church is also being plagued with numerous cases of ravenous deacons running wild in many churches, with some pastors not having the courage to act on the evil that is going on inside of their churches.

This decline in moral behavior in church leadership has gone from bad to worse in recent years, but we must continue to obey our church leaders and hold them up in prayer at all cost.

Keep in mind that there is good and evil in this world, and God will never let evil overcome good. Please just keep your faith in God and everything will work out fine.

Remember also that you must be a part of God's program, which is the local church, and this is not negotiable. True believers must be where the Word of God is being preached in the proper context and also where alike minds can form the truth of God's Word.

Please do not attend Saint Mattress or Bed Spring Baptist Church on Sunday mornings with a television preacher and call this church. You cannot cheat God.

Finding a Good Church

Again, finding a good church is not an option for Christians; we have to be a part of God's church. We also need to grow and build Godly character.

If I were to tell you that you just need to find a good Fundamental Baptist Church and you would be all set, I would be lying to you. The number one reason for writing this book is not to lie to you, but to help you find the truth. Please remember the following statement because you will need to understand this statement as you go through life: Some lessons in life must be learned and experienced, not all lessons in life can be taught. The same lessons that God has had for me will differ from the lessons that he will teach you.

The answer to finding the right church is to seek God's will and to be very careful in your selection. There will also be some Scriptures at the end of this chapter to memorize. Please study the Scriptures and seek the Lord in prayer while trying to find your new church.

The Parable of the Young Priest will also give you some insight to your question of finding a good Christian church.

Remember, a parable sometimes is the answer to a question asked.

The Parable of the Young Priest

WITHOUT LOVE, YOU HAVE NOTHING

In a far and distant kingdom, a young priest was in the process of completing his degree studies at a Worldwide Relationship Seminary. This year, an older priest, who had graduated in the past from the same Worldwide Relationship Seminary, was selected to come from another kingdom to preach the graduation service for this young priest and the many other young priests that were graduating that year. The older priest and his wife were treated like royalty during the weekend graduation services at the seminary that year. The old priest and his wife were both fed the best food that the seminary could provide to them. The wife of the old priest was also given many types of expensive flowers and was pampered by all of the women in the church congregation.

During graduation services, the old priest would preach hard on the problems facing the other churches in the kingdom and their need to use the proper Bible translation. The old priest would also attack some of the other churches in the kingdom as being too soft and not studying as hard as the Worldwide Relationship Seminary ministers studied. The young priest then suddenly looked around into the crowd and could see that the atmosphere in the church during the sermon by the old priest was turning very cold, but the old priest continued to hammer away at the poor doctrine and loud music at the traditional New Evangelical churches. After the sermon ended and the services had concluded at the Worldwide Relationship Seminary, the congregation walked out with a sense of pride as being the most educated sect of all of the churches in the kingdom, but the coldness in the church was again visible on the people's faces as they left the sanctuary. There were no smiles on the people's faces or no true love in their hearts. The people formed in their own little cliques, looked down on each other, and quickly went home.

Shortly after the graduation service, the young priest, now ordained as a Worldwide Relationship priest, made a vow in the church that one day, he would see the old priest to fellowship with him and his wife. The young priest was a man of great integrity and he knew from his intense training that once he made a vow in the house of the Lord, that this vow must be kept.

So the following year, the young priest, bound by his vow in the church, set out with his lovely wife to a distant land to honor the vow that he had made to the old priest. The young priest would now brave many obstacles to fulfill this vow to the old priest and also took time from his young priestly duties to make this long journey.

When the young priest finally reached his destination in the far and distant land, he immediately went to the old priest's church with his lovely wife. Upon their arrival, the old priest had almost no time to see the young priest because he was too busy preparing the Sunday morning message to his congregation just minutes prior to the Sunday morning services. The old priest's wife was also too busy to entertain the young priest's lovely wife because she was busy planning an afternoon church program.

The young priest and his lovely wife would then stay through all of the church services, hoping that they would get a chance to fellowship with the old priest and his wife, but felt a sense of coldness from the church members during the services.

Late in the afternoon when the church services were finally over, the young priest was informed by the old priest that he would be leaving to address another Worldwide Relationship Church and that he would be too busy to have dinner with the young priest and his lovely wife. The young priest was crushed, but the young priest remembered his priestly training on what happens when you put your faith in a man instead of God: you will get hurt every time.

Brokenhearted and rejected, the young priest journeyed far and long back to his home in a distant land.

Once at home, the young priest continued his priestly duties and worked hard in many Worldwide Relationship Ministries, but something was missing. All of the Worldwide Relationship Churches he was attending were turning so cold and impersonal.

The young priest and his lovely wife had noticed that right down the road from their house, a church was being built. The only problem about this new church that was being built was that the church was not a Worldwide Relationship Church. The young priest and his lovely wife were only use to attending Worldwide Relationship Churches with the high levels of teaching and the correct Bible translation.

But now the young priest was curious about this church, and one Sunday, the young priest and his lovely wife attended their worship services and found out that the church did not have the right Bible translation but the young priest had no problem following the service. The sermon was not preached with the heavy theological style of Worldwide Relationship ministers, but the evangelical preacher made some very good theological points. The young priest started to notice almost right away that this service was warm, and the women of the church accepted the young priest's lovely wife with open arms. The main difference between the Worldwide Relationship Church, which he was used to attending, and this new Church was that the people acted like they truly loved each other, and it was apparent in their interaction with them and with each other. When the young priest went home after the warm service at the new church, neither the young priest nor his lovely wife could believe that there was such a warm and loving congregation of people right down the street from their house.

The young priest remained a Worldwide Relationship minister, but he learned the most important lesson of his young priestly life.

This particular lesson could not be taught in the classroom or be taught by the many books that the young priest had read during the many years of his priestly studies.

The lesson now learned by the young priest was one of the keys to the Gospel of Jesus Christ. It is not about whom you may know in this world or what you may know in this world, but it is about the love that you show to God first and the many other people that you come in contact with in this journey we call life.

Chapter Two Summary

The local New Testament churches today have many different groups of people that are attending church every Sunday. As we discussed in chapter 1, evil is part of the reality of this world and the devil's people will be at church to meet you. The devil's people are one of the groups of people that are alive and well in your local churches. Please love them and everyone else you come in contact with, but beware of people and save your highest praise for God and not man.

As long as you keep your eyes on Jesus Christ, evil will never be able to harm you, and you will be able to grow with power into a child of God to be used for the Master and not by the pastor. Please keep Jesus Christ the main focus in your life. (More on this theme later.)

The search for the truth both begins and ends with the Lord fixated in your life or the forces of evil will find you and destroy your sense of purpose in the church.

I'm not trying to confuse you into thinking your pastor is not important, but the Master is what you need to strive to be like. The problems will come when you seek after man and find out that there is "spiritual wickedness in high places."

Summary of the Parable of the Young Priest

One of the keys of the gospel of Jesus Christ is a profound love for Jesus Christ first and then a true love for each other.

You can have the most theologically sound church in the world, but if there is no love for God first and no love for each other, you have nothing.

I have studied at the feet of some of greatest Bible teachers in this country and the need for love in your heart was taught to me time and time again.

Scripture Memorization:

> Trust in the LORD with all thine heart; and lean not unto thine own understanding. In all thy ways acknowledge him, and he shall direct thy paths.
>
> Proverbs 3:5–6 (KJV)

> Jesus said unto him, Thou shalt love the Lord thy God with all thy heart, and with all thy soul, and with all thy mind. This is the first and great commandment. And the second is like unto it,

Thou shalt love thy neighbour as thyself. On these two commandments hang all the law and the prophets.

Matthew 22:37–40 (KJV)

Jesus saith unto him, I am the way, the truth, and the life: no man cometh unto the Father, but by me.

John 14:6 (KJV)

Personal Study

If I speak in the tongues of men and of angels, but have not love, I am only a resounding gong or a clanging cymbal. If I have the gift of prophecy and can fathom all mysteries and all knowledge, and if I have a faith that can move mountains, but have not love, I am nothing. If I give all I possess to the poor and surrender my body to the flames, but have not love, I gain nothing. Love is patient, love is kind. It does not envy, it does not boast, it is not proud. It is not rude, it is not self-seeking, it is not easily angered, it keeps no record of wrongs. Love does not delight in evil but rejoices with the truth. It always protects, always trusts, always hopes, always perseveres. Love never fails. But where there are prophecies, they will cease; where there are tongues, they will be stilled; where there is knowledge, it will pass away. For we know in part and we prophesy in part, but when perfection comes, the imperfect disappears. When I was a child, I talked like a child, I thought like a child, I reasoned like a child. When I became a man, I put childish ways behind me. Now we see but a poor reflection as in a mirror; then we shall see face to face. Now I know in part; then I shall know fully, even as I am fully known. And now these three remain: faith, hope and love. But the greatest of these is love.

1 Corinthians 13:1–13 (NIV)

Salvation

A Case for Jesus Christ

For God so loved the world, that he gave his only begotten Son, that whosoever believeth in him should not perish, but have everlasting life.

John 3:16 (KJV)

In the world today, some people vary just by the color of their skin. Some people are short in stature, while others may be tall. But regardless to the color of one's skin or one's overall height, we all have something vastly in common. The one common denominator that links all of mankind is that every one of us on this planet has three distinct dates in life that we did not make for ourselves or we cannot break. The first date that all mankind shares in common is a date with death. One day, we are all going to die; this particular date is nonnegotiable and unavoidable. Man will have to die a physical death to rid ourselves from these fleshly bodies, and heaven will be our eternal home if we make the correct decisions during our lifetime here on earth. The second date that all of mankind shares in common is based on a decision that we all must make regarding where we want our individual souls and spirit to reside for eternity. Unfortunately, there are only two choices that you can make while you are still alive, which are heaven or hell. Please be advised that this second date is only negotiable while you are still alive because if you choose not to make this choice during your lifetime, you will automatically reside in hell. The third and last date that all mankind shares in common is also nonnegotiable; this will be a face-to-face meeting with our Lord and Savior Jesus Christ. At this meeting, unbelievers and the saints of God will be judged separately for what they did or did not do for Christ's kingdom during our earthly existence and also what rewards that will be given to each of us. If your decision is made not to follow Jesus Christ during your earthly existence, then your soul will be lost forever and a place called hell will be your new home. Again, this is just my own strong belief based on an absolute truth, which is the Word of God that is shared by many of other Christian brothers and sisters worldwide, and also numerous other Christian brothers and sisters throughout the history of the world. Yes, we all could be wrong, but I truly believe that this gamble is not worth sending your soul and spirit to a place like hell for eternity.

Besides, what is so bad about living a clean Christian life that offers you eternal life after death?

During your lifetime without Christian teaching, you will be involved with all kinds of negative virtues that this world will offer you, such as greed, drug abuse, sexual immorality, and a very unhappy lifestyle. You yourself are a witness to these negative virtues being played out on your television screen and also in your daily newspapers.

People in this world today, rich and poor, are catching hell during their earthly lives and then finding out when their lives are over that they do not have any retirement plan for their souls. This chapter is about choices. I know that you read the tabloids while you're waiting in the checkout lines at your local grocery store. I must ask you this question truthfully: Are the rich and famous really happy? If your answer is yes, then why are the people in Hollywood going in and out of rehab centers without making any real positive changes in their lives?

During this chapter, I am going to make a clear case for Jesus Christ to you in plain words. Also after reading this chapter, you will not be an authority on the concepts of Christian salvation, but this chapter can be a starting point for you to get on the path for further teaching at your local church. I will use the greatest testimony that I can give to you for my case for Jesus Christ, which is my own testimony on how I got saved. But first, let us look at what this word *salvation* means based on a dictionary interpretation. I will give my own interpretation of what salvation means to me later in this chapter.

The word *salvation* means to be saved from something, such as suffering or the punishment of sin. The next meaning for the word *salvation* is to be saved for something, such as an afterlife or participating in the reign of God. As I make a case for Jesus Christ in this chapter, we must understand that the cornerstone of Christianity is the love that Jesus Christ has shown for all of mankind, based upon our Scriptural reference of John 3:16, which is our main text. And if you think that the world was conceived by the big bang theory or that mankind has evolved from apes, please continue to the read this book, and hopefully, you will just look at yourself in the mirror and give up on these two senseless theories. Mankind was put here on this earth for a particular reason and was given careful instruction on how to live and how to interact with God and each other.

Our Lord and Savior Jesus Christ has written a book that has sold more copies than all of the Harry Potter books combined, and we can also throw in Dan Brown's *The Da Vinci Code* hundreds of times over. This book, the Holy Bible, has never gone out of style and continues to save people's souls today just like it has saved people's souls two thousand years ago. This book, the Holy Bible, which is one of the most read books in the world today and the bestselling book of all times, promises that if you follow Jesus Christ that you will live forever based upon something that Jesus Christ has already done for you. I would think that a rational person would read this book and find out what it was all about, especially when the world has no plans for your soul after death. I would think that people in this country would have no problem reading this great book that has changed billions of people's lives for the better, throughout the history of the world. I again would think that since every major crime statistic in this country continues to rise, brothers keep killing brothers, and mothers keep killing their babies that this book called the Holy Bible would be flying off the bookstore shelves, but it is not. The reason why this book, the Holy Bible, is on decline in most bookstores is that we live in a sick society where people are not seeking to read the truth. Most people in society today cannot handle the truth and want to believe lies rather than seek change for their lives.

Listed in this chapter are some reasons why people do not seek help when their lives are being destroyed. All of these principles will be taught in a deeper context in the next edition of this book, but this first book is a good starting place.

Now let us look at the three major forces in your life that are keeping you from the saving graces of God. The first force that is drawing a wedge between you and God is your inner self.

This inner self is called your flesh. The flesh is the inner you that is deep down inside your soul that just wants to be pleased. The flesh knows what is right and wrong, but just wants to be happy because it feels good.

Remember the analogy of the person that uses crack cocaine? He knows that using crack cocaine is wrong, but his flesh or inner self keeps him chasing that first high, which will never be a part of his reality again. Drugs, sex, and all kinds of immoral acts please the flesh, but never completely satisfy the flesh, and a person just keeps seeking to recreate these immoral acts for a short sense of happiness. You see, the flesh just wants to be happy, but is pleasing the flesh really happiness? I say no. This constant chasing for quick gratification for pleasing the flesh causes people to be put into bondage, and many people will lose track of reality. Are you really happy being strung out on dope? Is your definition of happiness spending all of your money on pornographic pictures?

Again, are you really happy having sex with several different women at the same time? The answer to all of the above questions must be no, but people continue to do all kinds of immoral things instead of trusting and relying in the truth of God's Word. When will people finally understand that there is no true happiness outside of a loving relationship with God?

This subject reminds me again about my friend Randy. Randy would quote Scripture when the words of the individual Scripture could be used to his advantage. This means that Randy had some sense of God's Word, but poor Randy would never read the entire Scriptures in the correct context to grasp the full truth of God's Word. Again, Randy is like millions of people in the world today who know that following Jesus Christ is the right thing to do, but put off their commitment to follow Jesus Christ until some great tragedy occurs in their lives. The problem with waiting to commit your life to Jesus Christ is that sometimes in life, things can happen to you, and you may never be able to make a commitment to Jesus Christ, and then your soul will be lost for eternity. What a waste because eternity is a very long time.

The second major influence that is being applied in the world today to stop people from pursuing the saving grace of Jesus Christ is the world's systems. The world's systems are people, powers, organizations, or anything that is out there in the world today that keeps you from giving your life over to Jesus Christ. The world's systems want you to think that you can have fun outside of giving your life to God. This false definition of fun is one of the main problems that are keeping you from being saved by the amazing grace of God.

Everyone in the world's systems just wants to have fun, based on the world's concept of what fun is. But in reality, people in the world's systems are not really having fun based on the truth. I have lived both lifestyles and I do not miss waking up sick from drinking booze all night long. I also do not miss waking up every Sunday morning not knowing how much money I wasted the previous night, trying to impress a bunch of people who really did not care whether I lived or died. I certainly do not miss waking up drunk with a strange woman in my bed on Saturday or Sunday mornings, not knowing how she got in bed with me or whether she may have just given me some disease that would kill me in this lifetime and also in the next life.

The point that I am trying to make here is that there is no fun in the world's systems today. The newspapers are full of stories of how the world's systems is collapsing into sex, greed, and declining moral behavior.

The tabloid press is also full of people who are multi-millionaires who are having behavioral meltdowns based on poor moral behavior and because they cannot find true happiness in their lives. I agree that today even the church is experiencing some of these same problems, but not at the magnitude that the world's systems are being affected. When will the people in the world's systems find out that there is no fun outside of a loving relationship with God?

The third major force that is keeping you from the grace and love of God is a very dangerous created being that we talked about earlier in chapter 1. I have devoted the first chapter of this book to the forces of evil, due to the enormous success that the devil and his crew are having in the world today. You see, my dear brothers and sisters, this place called hell was never meant for you or me, but hell was going to be the final resting place for satan and his fallen angels. When Adam and Eve brought sin into the world, after being deceived by satan himself, mankind would now be tainted by evil until this very day. The good thing about this whole process is that God loved mankind so much that he sent his only Son to ransom us from our sins and be a sin offering for all mankind. When the Lord Jesus Christ died for our sins, he spoiled the devil's plans of taking all of mankind to hell with him. We now have a choice whether we can have eternal life through the saving grace (free will) of Jesus Christ or join the devil in hell for eternity. As I have stated earlier, that salvation has already been completed when Jesus Christ died on the cross. Now all you need to do is make the decision to follow Jesus Christ to eternal life or follow the devil, the world's systems, and the flesh straight to hell.

This is why you must get under the authority of a good Bible-teaching church to constantly hear the Word of God and to know the truth. Since satan is the greatest liar in the history of the world, therefore you need to be constantly under the Word of God to keep you on the right path. Satan and his crew of fallen angels are very consistent and will keep trying to destroy the works of Jesus Christ because they know that their time is extremely short. The goal of satan now is to take as many of the

Lord's people to hell with him and his fallen angels. Also, we must remember that satan is a real creature that is in the world today, trying to stop you from the saving grace of God. I will address satan's schemes and methodologies later in this book in great depth.

Now it is time for me to give my own personal testimony about how I got saved and what salvation truly means to me. Every one of us that has been saved by the amazing grace of God needs to tell their own personal story to help other unsaved people to see the beautiful relationship that Jesus Christ has given to us.

Please enjoy this short biography of my life before and after I found Jesus Christ in my life. My prayer is that my biography on how I got saved will help to open some doors of truth in your life and help to point your feet on the right path. Please do not be like the old me that wasted years of time and thousands of dollars chasing happiness outside of a relationship with God. Amen.

The Melvin Wilson Story

How I Got Saved

Let the redeemed of the LORD say so, whom he
hath redeemed from the hand of the enemy.

Psalm 107:2 (KJV)

In the year of our Lord, on January 16, 1956, Melvin
Douglas Wilson was born into this world by a strong
and loving African-American mother and an abusive,
alcohol-addicted African-American father whom I
both loved. During the early 1950s, our small African-
American family unfortunately resided in the south end
of Springfield, Massachusetts. The Wilson family con-
sisted of my three older brothers: Leonard, Eric, and
Reginald, with my one and only baby sister Brenda. I
purposely noted that our family resided in the south end
of Springfield because during the early 1950s, the south
end of Springfield was home to mostly Italian-American
families. It is my strong belief until this very day that
God had his hand of protection on me way back in grade

school when the young Italian boys in the neighborhood would literally run my brother Reginald and me all the way home from school. I can still vividly remember the young Italian boys in our neighborhood yelling at us, "We are going kill both of you two niggers when we finally catch you!" The blessing was that the young Italian boys would never catch us because we could outrun all of the young Italian boys in our neighborhood. This ability to run faster than all of the boys in our neighborhood would keep my brother and me from a daily beating.

The Wilson family lived in an apartment building on 1121 Main Street filled with some other poor black families at the tip of the south end of Springfield. My father worked at the big Tire Company in Chicopee, Massachusetts, and had a deal with the owner of the tenement to do some cleaning in the building and to collect the trash in exchange for a break on the monthly rent. This sounded like a nice arrangement for our family, but my mother would always get stuck doing all of the work, due to my father going on numerous drunken binges. You see, my mother was a good Christian woman who kept our family together through her constant prayer and also by her close relationship with God. I never understood back then the power that we Christians have when you have a close relationship with God and the many doors that this relationship will open. I can remember the numerous times that my father would constantly drink up the rent money or owe most of his paycheck to the numbers man. It seemed like every payday, I can remember my mother going down to the local watering hole and pulling my father out of the bar. These were some very dark days for the Wilson family, but my mother would always find a way for us to get by.

Finally, after years of my father screwing up all of his money in the local bars, my mother would soon stop her total dependence on him and started working for an area doctor doing house cleaning.

During the early 1960s, my mother was keeping the apartment complex clean as well as working at the doctor's home and keeping our family going all at the same time. My mother was the hardest working person that I have ever seen because after a long day at work, she would always find the time to help us with our homework or to just joke around with all of her kids. My mother would also take a personal interest in both our schooling and moral upbringing. I can remember my mother sending my brother, sister, and me to a white Christian church every Sunday, which was now starting to plant the seeds of truth in my life. I can remember being picked up at nine o'clock every Sunday morning and also singing those good old-fashioned Christian hymns. Both my sister and I loved going to church on Sundays because it was a chance to be removed from the terrible environment where we lived, and also my sister and I were doing extremely well in the children's Sunday school classes.

This early exposure to attending church on a regular basis would soon come to an end when the church that my brother, sister and I were attending went through a split, and the church van no longer came to pick us up. The one positive thing that came from my first exposure to church was that the Scriptures and the hymns would still stay locked into my spirit for over thirty plus years, before I would ever cross the threshold of a church again.

Now, with the church experience behind me, I had to start looking for ways to make some money. The first job that I had was folding pizza boxes at Tony's Pizza in the south end of Springfield. I did not make a lot of money at the pizza parlor folding boxes, at a penny a box, so I started shining shoes in the local bars in the downtown section of Springfield. This extra money came in very handy because when I was growing up, our family did not have a lot of extra money for school clothes. But I can remember to this very day how my mother would keep the small amount of clothing that our family owned super clean, and she would iron all of our pants and shirts like they were a work of art, based on her training as a domestic worker. My teachers at school would constantly ask me who was ironing my shirts and pants to make them look so neat, and I would have the chance to say with pride that my mother ironed all of our family's clothing. To this very day, I press my own shirts and pants in a very tight crease and get the same compliments from people regarding the crisp creases in my clothing.

During the age of ten, I was doing just fine, but for some reason, you can always use a little extra money even when you are a kid. I guess this principle regarding money never changes: the more you get, the more you want. I soon would hit the jackpot and meet a Christian boy named Paul. Paul would put me in position to make mega bucks as a kid growing up in Springfield because Paul had the biggest newspaper route in the city and he would hire me to be his helper. You see, Paul was the son of the pastor of the Springfield Rescue Mission, and we became good friends right from the start.

This was a very successful period of life for me because I now had a good friend and was gainfully employed, but a bigger blessing was now yet to come. One day, Paul came to me and told me that his father was being transferred to a Midwest church and that I would now be in charge of his entire paper route. Paul would soon leave town and would truly be missed because he would be the last Christian influence in my life for a long time to come, other than seeing my dear mother constantly praying for our family and now going to church regularly.

During this time in my life, all I was thinking about was making money, and going back to church was not even on my radar screen. Besides, I now had the biggest paper route in Springfield, Massachusetts, and the money was rolling in, at the age of eleven. I kept this paper route for about two more years before our family moved to another area of Springfield. My mother had now quit her job working for the doctor cleaning his house and was working full-time at Northern Educational Systems, and she was also starting to go to school at night. As I look back at my mother's life now, I can see that my mother had truly found God in her life and the doors were now starting to fly open for her.

One of the doors that opened for my dear mother was that the Wilson family had gotten their first house in the black section of Springfield. I now had my own room, and I was starting to meet a few African-American boys in the neighborhood that were my own age. I was thirteen years old and also starting to look at the young girls in the neighborhood. My first girlfriend was a girl named Janice. Janice would also be my first sexual encounter; this early exposure to sex would put me on the road to destruction early in life.

During my junior high school years, all of the inner city African-American kids in our neighborhood were being bused to schools in the suburbs to provide racial balance in the city. The schools in the suburbs of Springfield were tremendously different than schools in our neighborhood because the suburban schools were all brand-new schools and had state-of-the-art learning centers built in them. Buckingham, the black junior high school where I was slated to attend, was now being closed for all kind of reasons: from having roaches in the classrooms to having below average test scores. Based on the quality of the poor inner city schools, the busing plan for the inner city kids was fair and reasonable because it put the inner city kids on the same playing field with our white brothers and sisters in Springfield. The only problem with the busing issue in Springfield was that where there is a positive reaction to a problem, a negative reaction can sometimes rear its ugly head.

The negative circumstance that the black students faced going into the suburban schools was that the parents of the white children in these schools did not want us to have a superior education, and sometimes, fights would erupt. The fights and racial slurs were a daily part of going to school, and this took away from the perfect environment of learning that suburban schools had to offer. During one of the many times of racial tension, a good old-fashioned fistfight would erupt in the hallways of the school, and many innocent victims were pulled into the madness of these terrible times.

I can remember roaming the hallway after an altercation with some of the bad white boys in the school, just looking for a white person to start some trouble with.

I managed to find an innocent white boy in the hallway and beat him up pretty bad. The problem was that the white boy that I beat up in the hallway was not one of the bad white boys that was starting all of the racial problems, but was one of the many good white people who were trying to help to get African-American brothers and sisters a better education in the suburban schools. After a suspension from the suburban junior high school, I had a chance to meet the family of the young white man, and this will always be one of the lowest points of my life. The two major lessons that I learned based on my senseless attack on this innocent young white man was not to judge a book by its cover and that all races have some good people and some bad people, and our main objective in life is to separate the good from the bad.

My mother would take this dark episode of fighting in school very hard, but she always gave me her relentless support, and most importantly, she always prayed for my success in the Lord. I was now finally kicked out of the good suburban school where racial tension sometimes outweighed the positive learning environment and put into an urban school for misfits with behavioral problems. Now, after serving six months in suspension school, I was going to another urban junior high school named Van Sickle.

During my short stay at Van Sickle Junior High, I would pick up every bad habit that would follow me throughout most of my adult life for years to come. My new crew at Van Sickle and I stole cars and used the money to buy booze and flashy new clothing. I was now starting to become a somewhat flashy dresser at school, and the little girls at Van Sickle Junior High School loved me. At least that is what I thought at the time, but the truth was that I was slowly going down the slippery slope of life and drowning all my sorrows in booze and drugs during my junior high school years. My mother, on the other hand, was now continuing to find God in her life on a full-time basis. I can remember this time very distinctly because God was continuing to open up so many doors for my mother. I can remember my mother was now starting college late in her life and also starting a new job in the Department of Social Service in Springfield.

For me, when I started high school, life did not change much from junior high; the only major difference was that now I was a chronic alcoholic and a petty drug dealer. While dealing drugs at Commerce High School, I was introduced to an older brother named Ralph. You see, Ralph had this huge connection for marijuana and pills with no distribution network. This is where I came into the picture. I was the man who handled the distribution and the networking. I had two other brothers working for me named GeGe and Clyde, which transformed us three brothers into an early version of the Cash Money Brothers (CMB).

As I now look back at my days in high school, I wish that I would have been more productive, and that I would not have wasted all of my time and energy on living this lie that I was having so much fun or that I was someone important.

I wish that I would have embraced the truth and hit the books because later on in life, I would have to spend thousands of dollars and a lot of time and effort to make up for my foolishness earlier in life. I spent my entire high school years just getting by, with no preparation for my future.

You see, Commerce High School was a business school, and me and my crew were play acting the part of young businessmen wearing shirts and ties to school. In reality, we were only just a bunch of dumb ghetto kids going nowhere fast. I see this same problem today with young kids not wanting to face the true reality that life brings them, and now end up going down nonproductive roads, just like I did. It seems that the devil creates a new bunch of lies for each new generation of ghetto kids, so that they do not reach their purpose in life.

The devil in his effort to corrupt ghetto children is not working alone. He is teaming up with non-caring parents, and with these two forces working together against this new generation of kids, they will not even stand a chance to have a better life. As I look back to my generation and also see this new generation of kids growing up, I can now see that the devil is still using the same old lies, just with a new twist. During my generation, the young kids in the ghetto neighborhoods wanted to be a bunch of drug dealers or pimps. This new generation of kids want to be rappers, drug dealers, or professional athletes. The main problem with believing these lies that satan is feeding these kids is that only less than a percentage point of young, poor ghetto kids will ever find any success in these areas, and being a drug dealer will definitely send them to jail fast. The question is what about the other 99 percent of the kids who do not make it to become a rap artist or a professional athlete? The other large percentage of kids will either end up in jail or at some dead-end job without the power of God working in their lives. We can also see another whole group of young kids failing due to the self-fulfilling prophesy, which is formulated by the constant efforts of the world's systems and the parents of these young ghetto kids relentlessly putting into their minds that they will not amount to much, and soon, they believe this lie, and the lie becomes their new reality. Now only a small percentage of our ghetto children beat the odds and climb out of this meat grinder without the power of God working in their lives, but this very small percentage of successful kids is already figured into the devil's plan.

Among other things, the devil is the world's greatest statistician. He is the one who has turned the biblical lot system into the lottery and has enslaved millions. (More on this in the next book.) Satan will always beat you with the odds in any given situation. The devil also excels at deception, lies, or your individual pride. You see, satan had me thinking that I was a big man at Commerce High, so I believed the illusion that I was having a whole lot of fun, and that I was someone important. Satan also had this pride thing working in me while I was watching all of the people standing outside my classroom, waiting for me to get out of class to sell them some drugs. I was a real big man, who was playing the fool. I just kept chasing this lie that I was this big businessman without any corporate headquarters or no real board of directors, other than the devil constantly cheering me on, telling me how smart I was.

The true reality of my senior year of high school is that I would graduate from Commerce High probably last in my class. I would be physically the last senior to leave the high school building after taking numerous makeup tests and special classes to graduate. I truly believe to this very day that the administration of Commerce High School was going to get me out of Commerce High School one way or another because they knew I was nothing but bad news. I finally would graduate from Commerce High with no hope for the future, no marketable skills after high school, and college was not even an option for me, due to all of my failing grades that I had received while at Commerce High.

I now had to find a job fast because after high school, my distribution network was gone. The first job that I found was working at an area aircraft manufacturing facility. The pay was good for an unskilled young black man in the Springfield area, and since I did not have a car, I could get to work by a public transit bus that would pick up people at Winchester Square in Springfield and bring us to work in East Hartford. These were some good times for me because I had a pretty good job for a young unskilled black man, and I was still also hustling drugs on the side.

The Years of Destruction

During the 1970s, I would be entrenched in the local bar scene, and this would become my same routine for the next twenty plus years of my life. I wished to God that I could have saved all of the money and the time that I spent chasing the revolving door of hope in the world's systems, where there is no hope for people.

After high school, it was all about pleasing myself and this sinful flesh with drugs, alcohol, and sex. During this time in my life, I prided myself with having sex with more than one girl at a time. I can even remember dating two girls in the same apartment complex on two different floors. As I now see things through the eyes of a sober Christian man, this was not a true definition of fun, but was a true definition of someone who was truly unhappy with life.

In contrast to my own self-centered behavior, my dear mother was growing enormously in her faith and was now a member of the first class of African-American social workers in the Springfield Welfare system. My mother was now attending college and also was beginning to establish herself as one of the women leaders at her church. My mother, who was now in her early fifties, was doing something that I could not even think of doing, due to my poor grades in high school, which was to graduate from college with near perfect grades. I, in contrast to my mother, was still going down the other road, which leads to death and destruction, with no hope in sight.

During the 1980s, life was more competitive on the nightclub circuit. You needed some type of edge that would make you stand out from the rest of the poor chumps in the streets. To finance this need to impress women for sex, I took on an additional part-time job to buy the sharpest clothing in Springfield and became a very well-dressed man. I would work full-time all week, but then I would drink and sell liquor part-time on the weekends for extra money.

One of my many mottos was that I liked liquor so much that I got into the liquor selling business. Also, with all of this access to liquor and drugs at my apartment, I was attracting women like honey attracts bees. I can remember having numerous girls waiting for me to come over to their houses when the nightclubs closed, to continue drinking, doing drugs, and having sex into the wee hours of the morning.

During the 1980s, I finally started finding love in my life for all of the wrong reasons, and for some reason, these relationships were never working out. I started the eighties looking to finally get out of the bar scene, but something was always pulling me back into this terrible world that I was living in. I had finally stopped doing the drugs because they were no longer fashionable, and the quality and quantities of the drugs that this new generation of dealers were giving you was just a plain rip-off.

On the other hand, during this same time frame, my mother was still excelling both spiritually and at the Department of Social Service where she worked. I can remember her taking night classes in graduate school, studying all weekend for her master's degree in Social Service from American International College in Springfield, which she would obtain at the age of sixty-four. My mother would write up all of her term papers and have my brother Reggie neatly type them. I truly believe now that seeing God work through my mother and being the recipient of all of her prayers is the reason for me becoming the Bible-believing Christian that I am today.

During the 1980s, my mother moved quickly through the ranks of the Social Service Agency in Springfield to become one of the first black supervisors of that agency prior to her retirement. My mother's accomplishments are too big to list in this small book, and her spiritual accomplishments at her church were also more extensive than her secular accomplishments. My mother was the church clerk at her church and worked at many other church-related organizations helping underprivileged people in the Springfield, Massachusetts, area for many years. My mother was also the world's greatest mom to all of her children.

During my mother's lifetime, I had the chance to see what the Lord will do in a person's life firsthand through watching my dear mother. If you will just trust and rely on the Lord Jesus Christ, the sky is the limit in your life. My mother was a woman who excelled based on the power of God working through her life and would be a great example for me when tragedy struck my life.

I had finally hit rock bottom and every relationship that I had was always ending in some turmoil. I was engaged to a few women who I loved very much, but I was finding out that most of the women that I was falling in love with, loved themselves and their children more than they loved me. I was just a boy toy to them.

These were some really lonely times. It got so bad that I was even doing dating through the newspaper, hoping to find a committed relationship that would last. But the shining star during these times was again my mother, who would always give me wise Christian counsel and a very compassionate ear when my numerous relationships with different women would always go bad. My mother was my rock, and now she was retired from the Social Service Agency and was working full-time in her church's office and other church organizations.

Sometimes when you think that you have reached rock bottom, you may have a little farther to fall. When my dear mother died in 1996, I was devastated with absolutely no one to lean on in this world. Now, for the first time in my life, no one was available to give me a sense of direction or wise Christian counsel for my life, which was now already out of control. I can remember not taking any time off work because I needed to stay as busy as possible to stop from breaking down and crying. After the funeral, I locked myself in a room and drank very heavily and demanded change from myself immediately. The question that I kept asking myself was what will I do now and how can I create positive change for myself?

This was the most terrifying experience that I have ever been through, but out of my mother's death, new life was starting to appear in me. The truth is that it took my dear mother's death to put me on the road to salvation. All of the years that I watched her life flourishing in the church suddenly flashed before me, and then two weeks after my dear mother died, I was sitting in the pews of

Saint James Baptist Church in New Britain, Connecticut. I was on the right road now.

Two of the members of Saint James Baptist Church who frequented a little breakfast restaurant that I ate at were always asking me to come to church. I had never taken their invitation seriously, but now that my mother was gone, my first thought was to start attending church and find myself a nice woman like my mother and create positive changes in my life.

The goal would be to establish myself in the church first and then find that nice woman, who I am married to right now. This goal did not work until I found Jesus Christ in my life first. I went to church and was saved by the grace of God for many years before God would finally send me my perfect soul mate. The proper order is to seek him first in all that you do and establish a true relationship with God, and only then will the doors start opening for you.

Now it has been ten plus years that I have been saved and I have overcome alcohol addiction, sex addiction, fits of rage, and also a whole lot of other real bad addictions that are too numerous to list in this book, all by the power of the Holy Spirit working in me.

All of these addictions that I overcame was not through a twelve-step program, but with a one-step program, which is faith in Jesus Christ. The easiest thing that I ever did was to get saved by God's grace. I heard the gospel message for years at Saint James Baptist Church, and one day, the Lord told me it was now my time to go down to the altar and devote my life over to him. I walked down to the altar crying, and this strange feeling came over me. All of the other people in the church were also crying for joy.

This whole process of being saved was very easy, it only took a few minutes, but when it was over, it was like a burden was now lifted off me and the worries about where my soul was going spend eternity was all over. Yes, getting saved was easy, but the daily walk with Jesus Christ would now be the hardest part. Since I gave my life over to the Lord, I have now acquired an associate's degree from Springfield Technical Community College.

I have completed my bachelor's degree in Industrial Technology, and I am also working on a second degree program at another area college studying drug, alcohol, and rehabilitation counseling. On the spiritual side of my education, which is very important, because the world is full of educated fools, I am currently studying theology at a Hartford area Bible Institute, and I have obtained two other degrees in theology at two other area Bible colleges. I am excelling both inside and outside the classroom in just a few years with the power of God working in my life.

My case for Jesus Christ is of course my own witness and also countless other people throughout history who are now excelling in life based on the power of Jesus Christ and the Holy Spirit. I am now married to a beautiful wife, who also had never been married before and is very compatible to me. We both were looking for something our entire lives and just couldn't figure out just what we were looking for, but we both found God, then miraculously we found each other. My wife and I make the perfect couple and are a tribute to what God can bring into your life, if you put him first in your life and trust in his Word.

I have lived in both worlds, and the world's systems will not make you truly happy. The world's systems will just provide a lonely environment to drown your sorrows in. A true Christian who lives by the Word of God can look anyone in the eye and tell him or her that they are truly happy living to the glory of God. As I stated before, this is the belief of many other happy Christians that truly love life and are living life to its fullest trusting in God and not the world's systems, the flesh, or the devil.

If you want to see the world's systems at work, just go down to your local convenience store, which is not so convenient any more with all of the scratch ticket addicts trying to find hope in a scratch ticket. Again, if you want to go see the world's systems at work, please go to your local liquor store and watch the people in the world's systems trying to find relief from their loneliness and suffering by purchasing cigarettes and booze. The problem with drinking booze is that it only masks your problems, and no matter how much booze that you drink, your problems will still be with you. I have also found that when you drink booze to try to rid yourself of problems, you can create two problems because now, without help, you will be both drunk and broke before long. The last example I want to bring to you is to go out one night to a nightclub or casino and watch the people in the world throwing away their hard-earned money trying to be happy.

When will people learn that the reality of the situation is that you cannot have true happiness outside of a relationship with Jesus Christ?

The defense calls another witness!

The Three Myths Keeping You from the Love of God

The number one myth that keeps people from the saving graces of God is money. You have heard people say, "I am not going down to that church and give these preachers my money," is the battle cry of most people, which is totally untrue. The money that a true Christian saves by not keeping up with the Joneses and not partaking in booze, drugs, hope in lottery, hope in scratch tickets, extramarital sex, clubs /casinos, plastic surgery, credit card/ debit card debt, and another endless list of other vices that the world pursues for their own self-gratification.

These vices in the world's systems and also pleasing to the flesh can cost some unbelievable amounts of money, but God can free you from these terrible vices if you will let him.

Today, I am a Bible-believing Christian and have no problem giving money to help the church and also to help people less fortunate. You see, now that I have stopped all of my old vices, I have additional money to enjoy life and travel the world. I also have money to put in the bank; this is something that I never could do before. Please do not believe the lies of satan concerning money being a problem if you start your walk with Jesus Christ. Because if you listen to the Lord and be obedient to the Word of God, you will have more money than you ever had in the world's systems and also live a better life.

The second myth that keeps people from the saving graces of God is the hypocrite principle. This principle helps you create in your mind this thinking that everyone down at the church is a bunch of hypocrites. These thoughts are being put in your mind by satan, your inner self "the flesh," and the world's systems to criticize the things of God to make you feel better about your own miserable life. A great illustration of this principle is our friend Randy, who could not find happiness in the world's systems, but looked hard to find faults with me being a Christian, so he could feel better about his own miserable existence. You see, Randy is like millions of people today who are drowning in the world's systems and fighting a losing battle to stop pleasing their fleshly desires. If your inner self and the world's systems can criticize the only place that you can get help, they can keep you firmly on the road to destruction.

Remember from earlier pages of this book that the inner self just wants to be happy and will destroy you in the process. Please do not fall for the hypocrite principle because the Bible tells believers that we are all a bunch of lost sinners saved by the grace of God, and when you join the church, you will just be another hopeless sinner added to the list. The difference now between you and the people that you leave behind in the world's systems is that you are now on the right path to recovery.

The third myth that keeps people from the saving graces of God is that most people think that Christians do not enjoy life. People think that Christians just go to church and read the Bible all of the time. This is another myth that is totally untrue because most people who are trapped in the world's systems are not going anywhere in the first place. When I was a hopeless sex-crazed alcoholic, I never traveled past Atlanta, Georgia. Now that I have found God and purpose for my life, I am starting to see the entire world.

Yes, I know that people in the world's systems are travelers, but when they travel, they still bring all their worldly vices with them (booze, gambling, sexual encounters, and arguing). Is this true enjoyment? I would say no. I find that most people in the world's systems who are traveling in most cases are just keeping up with the Joneses or just trying to only justify their own miserable lifestyles. As for reading the Bible, what are the people in the world's systems reading that is so important anyway, the Star or the National Inquirer or other gossip magazines? The Holy Bible is a great book that is the Word of God. This book can help you to be wise in all situations, and once you start reading the Bible, you will have the absolute truth of God's Word to apply to your life.

As I conclude my case for Jesus Christ to you, I pray with all of my heart and soul that no man or woman on the face of this earth perishes, but everyone will come to the knowledge of God. We are now at the crossroads of change in this country, and the devil, the flesh, and the world's systems are slowly stopping this nation from becoming the great Christian nation that God planned this country to be.

We are seeing a new generation of kids, both black and white, that are growing up in this country with no knowledge of God, and the moral fiber of this country is starting to unravel. I can remember when the crack cocaine epidemic raged through the black communities in the 1990s, and nothing was done about the carnage that crack cocaine inflicted on the African-American communities because it was just a bunch of them negroes stealing from their mamas and killing each other.

Today, this same crack cocaine epidemic is now in the suburbs along with other highly addictive drugs, which are taking a toll on what the media calls sleepy little towns "where this sort of thing never happens." The white community and its churches must be willing to invest into the black community to help stop the slide of moral decay in this country, because if we do not help each other, it will not be long before evil will start to move into a community near you. Remember, the devil is all for equal opportunity when it comes to getting people to join him in a place called hell!

As I make my final case for Jesus Christ, who is the only answer to all of our problems, please believe that God has hard wired every one of us to know that there is a God in this vast universe. Our only problem is that sometimes we cannot understand where he resides. I beg you, my brothers and sisters, to get yourself to a Bible-believing church and hear the truth of God's Word, which will help to create your faith in God. Please draw near to the Lord and he will also draw near to you.

The Lord has given mankind free will from the beginning of time. God loves us all and wants everyone to be happy, productive members of the kingdom of God.

Please look at yourself in the mirror today, and ask yourself the following questions, and be honest with yourself concerning your answers to these questions.

1. Am I truly happy in life today?

2. Why am I having problems finding a mate?

3. Could I bring Jesus Christ to the places that I frequent?

4. Why am I putting all of my hope in lotto, casinos, and gambling?

5. Why am I having problems with relationships with other people?

6. Why can't I quit alcohol or substance abuse?

7. Why am I not very successful at work?

8. Why is my marriage falling apart?

9. Why am I broke and continuing to have money problems?

10. Why is it when I try to do the right things, something is constantly holding me back?

As I rest my defense in my case for Jesus Christ, if you need help with any of the ten questions above, Jesus Christ can make a change in your life.

I continue to literally beg anyone who is reading this book to give Jesus Christ a chance to work in your life. Yes, you will have problems going forward, but you will not have to face these problems alone, and you will never be lonely again. Also, you will now be on the road to eternal life through Jesus Christ our Lord.

Again, please get to a Bible-believing church and start putting your life under the authority of God, and today, start adopting a happy Christian lifestyle.

> Who comforteth us in all our tribulation, that we may be able to comfort them which are in any trouble, by the comfort wherewith we our-

selves are comforted of God. For as the sufferings of Christ abound in us, so our consolation also aboundeth by Christ.

2 Corinthians 1:4–5 (KJV)

For God so loved the world, that he gave his only begotten Son, that whosoever believeth in him should not perish, but have everlasting life.

John 3:16 (KJV)

The thief cometh not, but for to steal, and to kill, and to destroy: I am come that they might have life, and that they might have it more abundantly. I am the good shepherd: the good shepherd giveth his life for the sheep.

John 10:10–11 (KJV)

Melvin's Definition of Salvation

Salvation is displaying the abundant power of God's grace, operating in an individual during his lifetime here on earth, for the good of his new master the Lord Jesus Christ first, and also for the good of his world community prior to leaving for his eternal home in heaven.

Conclusion

Becoming a Christian was one of the easiest things that I ever accomplished in my life after I removed all of the roadblocks that were keeping me from getting to God's grace. I can remember reasoning that I was not going to run down to these churches and give away all of my money to these church leaders. This type of reasoning was not only very selfish, but it was not true. When I started going to church seriously, I was saving thousands of dollars that I was not drinking up every weekend, thinking that I was having fun. This clean Christian lifestyle has helped me to save enormous amounts of money and enjoy life even after contributing handsomely to my local church and supporting people in the community.

The easy part comes when you first get saved, but the hard part comes sustaining your Christian lifestyle over time. Almost immediately, you will find the world's systems trying to pull you back, your flesh wanting to be pleased again, and the devil constantly telling you that following Jesus Christ is not worth the effort. During your young Christian life, a battle is going to be waged for your soul, but you can overcome all of these obstacles. Please stand firm in God's Word because it will not be long before you will now start to see life more clearly, and God's Word will start to change your heart. Soon, the process of God's grace will start to change your lifestyle from negative to positive, and it will not be long before you will be ready to be used by Jesus Christ for great things, if you can stay on the right road. You see, true Christians do not have any problems regarding being unsure that if we die today, where our souls are going to spend eternity. Again, Jesus Christ can give you the ability to be sure that heaven will be your home after you die, and also that while you are still alive today, that you will be both happy and productive right here on earth now.

With Jesus Christ, you can beat all of the odds. The devil just wants you to roll the dice (law of probability). The house always wins. Hell is your new home!

The world's systems has no plans for you, but to have fun while you're still alive. No retirement plan for your soul. Hell is your new home!

The flesh just wants to be happy because it feels good and does not care if you end up dead. No retirement plan for your soul. Hell is your new home!

Please give your life over to Jesus Christ today. He cares, and you will never be sorry that you did.

The defense will now rest his case.

Faith

Pleasing God

Now faith is the substance of things hoped for, the evidence of things not seen.

Hebrews 11:1 (KJV)

During your Christian walk with God, one of the most important words that you will need to embrace is the word *faith*. You see, in order to build a solid relationship with God, all believers must firmly believe in the nature of God and also believe that God can do whatever he says he will do. This faith that you have in God must be unshakable or the constant trial and tribulation from the three enemies that we discussed in earlier chapters will turn you away from God.

The Bible tells believers in Ephesians 2:8–9: "For by grace are ye saved through faith; and that not of yourselves: it is the gift of God: Not of works, lest any man should boast" (KJV). This Scripture can best be interpreted as saying that the grace that comes from our loving God has been given to mankind as a free gift or unmerited favor. You will not get to heaven and see anyone boasting how they got there outside of believing in Jesus Christ.

My dear brothers and sisters, this grace that our loving God has lavished on us cannot be purchased with money, nor can you work harder than the next person at your Church to achieve God's grace. Lastly, you cannot achieve this grace by becoming God's special person because God is not a respecter of any individual person.

We now need to be very clear and examine what makes God happy because your main goal in life should be to please God and not man. Faith is the main thing that pleases God. The Bible tells believers in Hebrews 11:6, "But without faith it is impossible to please him: for he that cometh to God must believe that he is, and that he is a rewarder of them that diligently seek him" (kjv).

Next, let us look at some people who pleased God and displayed tremendous faith according to the Holy Scriptures, which got God's attention. Such as Noah, who built an ark on dry land because it had never rained before on the earth. Noah would go on to save his entire family based on his faith. But he could not save the sinful people laughing at him, building this ark that God had instructed him to build. You see, Noah believed God and not man. This is what got God's attention. In addition to Noah, we can note that Abraham also believed God, when God told him to go into a land that he had never seen before and his people would be a blessed nation. The Bible also tells the story of the harlot Rahab whose entire family did not perish because she trusted in the God of Israel.

You will have to get further training on other people of faith at your local church, but you do see the pattern on how every person in the Bible who got God's attention was by showing their faith in him.

I have always said that grace is a free gift, based on the truth of the Scriptures, but the cost of following Jesus Christ is always down the road. Once you truly make up your mind to follow Jesus Christ, the battle for your soul will begin and your faith will constantly be tested.

During your Christian walk, your faith in Jesus Christ will constantly be challenged to display behavior that is not in the norm of this sick perverse society that we now live in. We as Christians should always be looking at things eternal or to the big picture of things, which glorifies God and not man. Again, one must understand that these things concerning following Jesus Christ will not be popular in this present world environment, and you will be laughed at and scorned similar to Noah building the ark on dry land. Even during the earthly ministry of Jesus Christ, he was also mocked and laughed at, so what makes you think that you will be any different? The good thing about Jesus Christ is that he would go on to change the entire world, despite the laugher of the crowd. Never listen to the crowd.

The Bible describes Christians in 1 Peter 2:9, "But ye are a chosen generation, a royal priesthood, an holy nation, a peculiar people; that ye should shew forth the praises of him who hath called you out of darkness into his marvellous light" (KJV).

Maybe you will move forward in the things of God and claim him and his power for your life, or maybe you will just be content being a person of little faith and sitting in the same pew going through the religious experience? This is your call.

I can only give my own testimony, and I will choose the Lord every time.

Melvin's Faith Tests

I can remember my first faith test as a young Christian, shortly after I got saved in 1998. At that time in 1998, I was working two jobs and doing very well financially. My full-time job was at a local manufacturing facility making aircraft parts, and my second job was in New Britain, Connecticut, at an area liquor store selling alcoholic beverages and lottery tickets. When I first got saved, I had no problems working at the liquor store part-time, but as my relationship with Jesus Christ got stronger, the job at the liquor store started to become increasingly a greater burden on my life.

Soon, the pastor of the church that I was attending at that time asked me if I wanted to join the usher ministry at church, and I accepted this very humble position. I was very excited about putting on my black usher suit and standing in front of the doors of the church, greeting people as they came into the sanctuary area.

I was a very faithful usher, who both looked and dressed the part. As time went on, the Holy Spirit was now starting the internal process inside of me, and it soon got very hard to represent both a Godly character at the church and represent the devil selling liquor and lottery tickets at the store part-time.

The Bible tells us in Matthew 6:24 that "No man can serve two masters: for either he will hate the one, and love the other" (KJV).

This Scripture will always come into play in your life when you try to put anything ahead of your relationship with God, and it will then boil down to whom do you want to serve: the devil, money, or possibly your fleshly desires?

This question will be asked repeatedly in your Christian walk, so get ready. Again, we have the free will to make these choices, but once the power of God's Word truly gets into your heart and the Holy Spirit becomes a stronger influence in your life, then change can truly occur in your life.

I would soon start to detest working at the liquor store because the Holy Spirit was now making working there very uncomfortable for me. Before long, I had done something that I could not have ever accomplished before alone, but with the help of the Holy Spirit working in me, I had completely stopped drinking alcohol. I had tried to quit drinking alcohol numerous times in my life before, but this time it was somewhat different for some reason. This time, I quit drinking, and I had no cravings for alcoholic beverages at all. It was like the Lord had taken the taste for alcohol out of my system, and this addiction to alcohol had been removed from my body. I had been enrolled in a twelve-step program to quit drinking alcohol many different times before, but this new one-step program, which was total faith in Jesus Christ, was now truly working. It would not be long before the Holy Spirit convicted me so badly at the liquor store that I would submit my resignation to the owner of the liquor store.

I can remember the day of my resignation: a voice in my mind clearly said to me, as clear as a bell, "You will never have to work a part-time job ever again." To this very day, I have never worked part-time or drank another drop of alcoholic beverages ever again. Praise the Lord.

It has been many years since the first test of faith in my life, and the Lord has always been faithful to me. The Lord would even exceed my expectation and bless me with a huge job later that year in the aircraft industry that I was totally unqualified to have, due to not having a college degree.

But now, I was starting to clearly see that in order for some things in this world to live, sometimes, some things in your life have to die in order to plant a lasting seed in you. I believe that seeing my dear mother succeeding by the power of God in her life was now having a positive effect on my own life.

The job that the Lord had given me had an above average pay scale and an educational assistance program to help me to pay for the numerous college degrees that I would go on to achieve from two secular colleges, and two local Bible Colleges. One would now think that all would be well, but remember that the cost to follow God will always increase. How you react to these choices, based on your faith, will determine your future blessing. I have seen many people in Christendom struggling year in and year out, based on not having the faith to believe that God will always do what he says he will do.

To all my brothers and sisters out there in Christendom, "God will not be mocked." The biblical law of reaping and sowing is not just a theory or a hypothesis, but a true law in the spiritual realm. Please put your faith in God, for this is the only way to please him.

During the 2009 recession, businesses in this country changed their philosophy in the way they were doing business, and the current labor force in the United States of America is now being used like disposable razors.

Mostly all of the companies here in the United States maximized their profits and used the recession as a reason to get rid of unproductive workers (to take out the trash) or to farm out their work to low-cost suppliers (China/ Eastern Europe) based on good old-fashioned greed. The world would change during this time in history, and our labor force in this country is being asked to do more or to look for another job elsewhere. The major problem with looking for another job elsewhere was that there were no other jobs elsewhere, and the management of these American companies knew this.

The hours were increased in the work week at most American businesses, and they now want you to be connected to their companies by laptop, Blackberries, and if necessary, some businesses even want you to text your boss 24/7. Soon major segments of the recession would end, but the demand to push workers would not end, and even working Sundays would not be taken off the table in many companies in this great Christian nation of ours. God forbid.

I have seen companies go from work-life balance to run their employees into the ground, and if you do not like the company's way of doing business, you could quickly walk out one of the doors or you could crawl out of one of the windows of their business. You just needed to leave peacefully because you cannot stay employed here at this company anymore. I am glad that my trust is in the Lord. The Lord "will never let the righteous fall." He is also a revealer of secrets, and he will share these secrets with you if you have a relationship with him. It is not just about showing up to church; it is about a relationship based on faith in him.

Please be advised that no true man of God will ever be ignorant of the plans and devices against him. I could clearly see that there would be a time coming down the road, in which I would have to choose who I would serve, and the Lord had been preparing me for that day well in advance.

The Lord gave me the wisdom to start putting my money in the bank and also to pay down all my bills prior to any decisions that were being made. I was even stocking up with extra underwear, shirts, and socks. I was like Noah, who knew the flood was coming, and I just had to trust God. I knew that God was not happy with my present job that was squeezing all of the strength out of me and making all types of demands on my time after work hours and also keeping me away from the Word of God.

During the very end of my time with this local company that preached work-life balance, I was not enrolled in a single Bible college class or reading my Bible at night, most of the time as a result of the 24/7 work environment that they created by not hiring enough people to maximize their profits. I was basically walking around like a zombie from day to day, and the little free time that I had over the weekend was being spent to rest up for the upcoming week. During the last days at this company, before my final departure, my blood pressure was in the range of a person just asking for a stroke, and my heart was beating rapidly at times. I was informed by my doctor that I was a walking heart attack just waiting to happen. My doctor would then put me under his immediate care, which I believe saved my life. Praise the Lord.

My dear brothers and sisters, if you do not stand up for God, you will fall for the devil's tricks every time and may miss your blessing. When a decision finally had to be made who would be the Master of my life, my decision was to follow the Lord Jesus Christ without a doubt. I can remember the Holy Spirit did all of the talking at the final meeting at work, and I did not have to say a word. The Lord would then go on to remove me very quickly from the company with an early retirement, and the Lord would then put me on a new assignment to write this book.

As we discussed previously, the faith test only increases during your walk with Jesus Christ, but the reward and the blessings will also increase. You see, if I win one person over to Jesus Christ with this book, it will be well worth all of the hard work and sacrifice it took to produce this book.

My dear brothers and sisters, I can tell you one thing upfront, and it is that this book is not going to go over well with the devil and his people and also the world's systems, but you cannot please these people and keep

God happy. Once you get saved, your main concern is to please God, based on your faith in him.

My prayer is that you will come through all your trials and tribulations with a strong bond with God and a positive relationship with our Lord and Savior Jesus Christ. Please keep your eyes fixated on Jesus Christ, not moving from the right or to the left.

If your chances don't look good in life, keep your eyes on Jesus Christ. Do not quit. The Lord, based on your faith, can change things around in the twinkling of an eye as the result of putting your faith in him.

If the entire world's systems and the devil want to take God's Word away from you, please keep your eyes on Jesus Christ. Do not quit. The Lord, based on your faith, can work all things for good in your life, based on your faith in him.

If your flesh just wants to have fun and ruin your life, please keep your eyes on Jesus Christ. Do not quit. The Lord, based on your faith, will put you in a one-step program, which is based entirely on the faith you have in him.

Now, we will have a short essay concerning this chapter. Remember, faith requires your total focus on God!

On the next page is a short essay regarding something I experienced prior to getting saved by the grace of God. You see, sometimes when you are even out there in the world and are unsaved, you can experience some things, and now that you are saved by the grace of God, you can see these things clearly through spiritual eyes. This is one of those moments. I purposely did not create this story in parabolic form because I need for you to clearly see how we all sometimes take our eyes off of the prize in this fast-paced world that we live in.

I continue to exhort my brothers and sisters throughout this book to keep your eyes on Jesus Christ, and my hopes and prayers is that this essay will help you to paint a vivid picture in your mind of how important it is to keep your focus on him.

Keeping Your Eyes on the Prize

During the early 1990s, prior to getting saved, I found myself in one of my more familiar settings during the course of my life here on earth under the sun, which was working again part-time at a liquor store in the south end of Springfield, Massachusetts. The old neighborhood that I had grown up in during my childhood had now become a very depressed area of Springfield, Massachusetts, with drugs and crime everywhere. I can vividly remember growing up in this area of the city in the late 1950s with only just a handful of African-American families, and mostly Italian-Americans living in this area, but oh, how times have changed in my old neighborhood. These same changes have also occurred in most neighborhoods in this country. The south end of Springfield, which was predominately Italian, is now the home to mostly poor African and Hispanic-Americans, with only a few poor white people in the mix, and almost no Italian-Americans now live in the south end of Springfield.

The owner of the liquor store where I worked part-time was named Jimmy, and he lived in the suburbs, but came into the inner city to seek the American dream. I guess the American dream for Jimmy was the lucrative business of selling hope to a bunch of poor, low-life people in the depressed area of the city in the form of alcoholic beverages and lottery tickets. This was how Jimmy would envision the people in this neighborhood and is not part of my thought pattern regarding underprivileged people.

Remember to all of you gamblers, all games of chance are primarily designed by the devil and the odds are against you before you ever start playing any of these games. Your chances to prosper and be successful monetarily playing any of these games are probably slim to none. The great statistician, the devil, will always be the only winner in the end (More about this subject in the next book.)

It was at this liquor store, I would have the chance to see unfold one of the greatest lessons to be learned in my entire life, which was to always keep your eyes on the prize at all cost. You see, when you take your eyes off the prize, you will always lose.

At the liquor store, Jimmy was the main boss, and like millions of other bosses across this great country of ours, Jimmy thought he knew everything and his poor workers knew absolutely nothing. I would constantly warn Jimmy of things to come, but he would just smile and never truly listen to my input because who was I anyway? Jimmy thought. I had a full-time and part-time job, but I was still just another one of them poor minority homeboys living in the hood.

In Jimmy's mind, the only reason that he hired me was to keep the locals happy, and that he needed someone to keep an eagle eye on his products, which were the alcoholic beverages in the store.

One day, Jimmy had brokered this huge deal to buy this cheap vodka that was not selling well at the liquor distribution center because it was probably not fit for human consumption. Jimmy, on the other hand, only saw huge dollar signs and believed that he had just the right place to sell this cheap liquor, which was to the urban low-life clientele that Jimmy catered to everyday. Jimmy would go on to buy out the entire stock of this cheap liquor from the liquor distributor, and he would then declare a major victory in his mind, based on the low cost that he purchased the liquor for and the extremely high profit margin on this cheap liquor.

Jimmy brought me into his office one day, smiling from ear to ear, as he explained the great amount of money that he would make on this big liquor deal and stated boldly that these bums will buy this cheap liquor and not even know the difference. I told Jimmy that it was a very risky investment, but Jimmy got mad at me and basically told me, "This is the reason you work two jobs and do not have your own business, Melvin." I can also still hear his words ringing in my head, saying, "Melvin, to be successful in business, you have to take risks."

I would again take a deep breath and once again warn Jimmy not to buy this cheap liquor because it wasn't ethically the right thing to do. Unfortunately, the dollar signs had already clouded Jimmy's thinking, and the huge savings was now also calculated in Jimmy's family budget. I never did get the final numbers, but the profit margin for this low-grade vodka must have been huge. When the liquor shipment finally came into the store, Jimmy said that he didn't sleep a wink that night and he wanted to get these pints and half-gallon bottles of this liquor up onto the shelves immediately. As soon as his first hardcore alcoholic customers hit the door, Jimmy was in their face asking them to buy this low-grade vodka, but for some reason, they were not interested. I watched intently at my perch in the corner of the store, which I used to keep an eagle eye on the movement in the store.

I began to see customer after customer shake their heads day after day when Jimmy would approach them about purchasing the cheap liquor. Jimmy would bend their ears and harp on the incredible savings on pints and the half-gallon sizes, but no one was biting. Jimmy would sell only a few pints of this liquor only sporadically, but for some reason, Jimmy never would get many return customers for this brand of cheap vodka.

Before this business venture was over, Jimmy would learn many valuable lessons regarding this big business deal of his. The major lessons learned by Jimmy was that people in a depressed area of the city may be poor and may not be Rhodes scholars, but one thing is for sure that even in the depressed area of the city, people do not want to be made a fool of and are not entirely stupid or ignorant.

When I had the chance to interview some of Jimmy's hardcore customers, they knew more about cheap vodka than I did. They knew about this particular brand of vodka, where it was made, and how it was made. I was impressed with the people's knowledge of alcoholic beverages, but I guess this is what an alcoholic does day after day; he should know about the product he is consuming, but Jimmy did not see things that way.

At this point, my man Jimmy was now getting worse day by day, due to the fact that the poor quality liquor was now not flying off the shelves as he had envisioned, and now he wasn't even getting any repeat customers.

Jimmy soon started taking out all of his unhappiness on his poor loyal customers because the profit stream from this rotgut vodka was now drying up and all the upfront money he paid to the liquor distributor was now cutting into his weekly profit. Soon, Jimmy was yelling at everyone who came into the store for just any little thing due to his unhappy demeanor.

I had a good friend and a very loyal customer who came into the store named Juan the Can Man. Juan would collect cans all day long and come into the store late every evening and reclaim the empty cans for five cents per can on the honor system, which Jimmy had implemented to teach the low lives in the community the value of being honest. Juan put his cans on the back counter and told Jimmy that the total was $2.60. Jimmy gave him the money and ran to the back of the store and counted the cans and found out that the tally was only $2.45.

Jimmy was now irritated with just about anything because of his failed business venture that went bad. Jimmy then cursed poor Juan the Can Man out, calling him some very choice words I would not like to print in this book, all over the 15 cent difference in the refund cost, and would now vow to get even with poor Juan. I had told Jimmy that we needed another person at night to keep an eye out on the refundable cans and to work in other critical areas of the store, but this request was just another one of my ideas that fell on deaf ears.

The next day, Jimmy had this great idea to put up a visual display in the front of the store and to discount all of the liquor at bargain basement prices. I warned Jimmy about the location of the display in the front of the store, but Jimmy insisted that we would "keep our eyes on the prize" and sell all of this low quality liquor once and for all and still make a good profit in the end.

Jimmy would then take the entire stock of the liquor and put it in the front of the store in a beautiful display to attract the eyes of people coming into the store. Jimmy again started pushing the poor quality liquor to all of his hardcore vodka customers who hit the door, but the liquor still was not selling. The display now had the entire stock of the liquor that was left in the store, and Jimmy wanted all of the stock to be sold as quickly as possible.

It was getting late in the shift and Jimmy had only sold one pint of the cheap liquor off the new display counter sitting in front of the store on wheels. Suddenly, Juan the Can Man had just opened the front door and Jimmy was looking for someone to take his wrath out on. Juan went quietly into the back room with an entire shopping cart full of cans. I immediately looked at Jimmy's face and he had just turned bright red as he said to me, "Melvin, I am tired of these poor bums stiffing me. I am going to go back there and count all of the cans myself." I told Jimmy that he was the one who implemented the honor system, and Juan was a good guy who was just down on his luck.

I told Jimmy that Juan may have not known that he messed up on the count last time. Suddenly, Jimmy exploded and said, "Who do you work for, me or Juan? These guys are constantly trying to screw me out of all of my money." Jimmy then yelled at me to come on and go to the back of the store with him. "I will show you that this Juan is a crook and it will only take a few minutes."

I told Jimmy that maybe I should stay out front, but he was now foaming at the mouth and was going show me to be wrong at all cost and also show me that he was so much smarter than me. Again I told Jimmy, "I will wait here," but he insisted that I go in the back of the store with him to check the count on poor Juan's cans.

Juan the Can Man was now finishing up when Jimmy and I both came into the back room, and he told Jimmy, "I had a very good day today, my refund will be $3.15." Jimmy said to Juan, "Not that fast, let me recount your cans."

Now Juan was very offended because Jimmy had told him about his honor system and Juan had thought Jimmy was a great guy for trusting the people of this poor neighborhood and treating them with a little dignity. Unfortunately, this time, Jimmy was right again when he second-guessed Juan. The new count of the refund was $3.05 as Jimmy recounted the cans; poor Juan had been off by ten cents. Jimmy screamed at Juan at the top of his lungs on how this was just like committing robbery and how he had trusted him in the past.

Jimmy told Juan the Can Man how his last count was also wrong and that this little money adds up! I felt so sorry for Juan and I truly believed it was only an oversight on his part. Jimmy finally told Juan to never come back to his store and was very verbally abusive to him.

At this point, all of the damage had now been done. Jimmy and I came out of the back of the store to the front of the store as Jimmy was now beaming from ear to ear telling me intently, "I told you Melvin that Juan was a crook." I had to acknowledge that Jimmy was finally right this time; Juan was off on his count.

We were now starting to get settled back into our spots in the front of the store, and we both started to notice that something now looked very strange. There was a big hole in the floor that just did not look right, and soon, both of our minds clicked at the same time. The entire display of low quality liquor that Jimmy had invested so much of his own money had been rolled out the front door while Jimmy was worried sick about Juan the Can Man robbing him of a grand total of 10 cents.

Now Jimmy had just lost his entire stock of the rot-gut vodka and the entire revenue stream that this cheap vodka would have generated. I couldn't believe it! We took our eyes off the prize for only a few moments and the entire stock of liquor was gone. Jimmy was very angry that day and would later go on to sell the liquor store and move into another line of business. But he would never forget this real big business deal of his.

Jimmy would probably never forget Juan the Can Man either. The word on the street was that Juan and his buddies set up the whole deal to teach poor Jimmy a lesson.

I never forgot this lesson, and neither should you. When I got saved, the Lord brought this lesson back to my remembrance many times over, based on the spiritual truth of this story. Now I try to never take my eyes off the prize, which is in Christ Jesus, because you can miss your blessings chasing the little things in life.

Chapter Four Summary

In today's world, everyone has to have faith in something. The people of this great country need to have faith that the senators, congressmen, and the president of the United States will do their jobs properly. At your place of employment, you need to have faith in the upper management structure to do their jobs properly. But we are now seeing good old-fashioned greed running wild in most businesses in this country (more in the next book.)

Most businesses in this country want to do more with less and maximize profits at all cost, while stripping their employees of any work-life balance and spiritual growth.

In the spiritual realm, both faith and spiritual growth are gravely important to a lasting relationship with God.

The Bible tells believers in Hebrews 11:6, "But without faith it is impossible to please him: for he that cometh to God must believe that he is, and that he is a rewarder of them that diligently seek him" (KJV).

In chapter 4, we looked at some people who pleased God in the Holy Bible, and the common theme of all of these men and women were that they all were looked upon as being weak and foolish from a worldly perception. You will also be perceived by the world's systems as weak and foolish as the trials and tribulations of following Jesus Christ increases. The good thing about following Jesus Christ is that as your trials and tribulations increase, your blessings will also increase. The trials and tribulations from a loving God are not applied to hurt you, but to help you become a better person and an ambassador for Jesus Christ here on earth.

Keeping Your Eyes on the Prize

The spiritual concept of keeping your eyes on the prize is one of the themes of this book. Please do not take your eyes off your relationship with Jesus Christ or you will lose every time.

In this essay, the story was slightly exaggerated to give you a more vivid picture in your mind of what this author needed to accomplish. However, the story is very accurate. This essay needs to be visualized properly and read by both young and mature Christians alike because we all need to keep our eyes on the prize in Christ Jesus. The names in this essay were also changed to protect the innocent.

The harsh language was a true perception of how Jimmy perceived poor and uneducated people, but is not the thinking of this author. This author does not look down on poor people or anyone else but loves everyone.

Spiritual Laws

In the world that we live in today, we have physical laws that are applied to our universe, which can govern our world around us such as gravity.

If you throw a quarter up into the air anywhere in the world, the quarter will fall from the air back into your hand based on similar conditions, every time and any place in the world consistently. Gravity is what also causes apples to fall from the trees and not suspend in midair.

God also has spiritual laws that govern his relationship with us. There are three spiritual laws listed below in the Scripture memorization.

1. "But without faith it is impossible to please him" Hebrews 11:6 (KJV). This is a biblical law.

2. "Now faith is the substance of things hoped for, the evidence of things not seen" Hebrews 11:1 (KJV).

3. "And almost all things are by the law purged with blood; and without shedding of blood is no remission" Hebrews 9:22 (KJV). This is a biblical law.

4. "But this I say, He which soweth sparingly shall reap also sparingly; and he which soweth bountifully shall reap also bountifully" 2 Corinthians 9:6 (KJV). This is a biblical law.

5. "Looking unto Jesus the author and finisher of our faith; who for the joy that was set before him endured the cross, despising the shame, and is set down at the right hand of the throne of God" Hebrews 12:2 (KJV).

6. "If the world hate you, ye know that it hated me before it hated you. If ye were of the world, the world would love his own: but because ye are not of the world, but I have chosen you out of the world, therefore the world hateth you. Remember the word that I said unto you, The servant is not greater than his lord. If they have persecuted me,

they will also persecute you; if they have kept my saying, they will keep yours also. But all these things will they do unto you for my name's sake, because they know not him that sent me." John 15:18–21 (KJV)

Sanctification

The Process of Becoming More Like God

Having therefore these promises, dearly beloved, let us cleanse ourselves from all filthiness of the flesh and spirit, perfecting holiness in the fear of God.

2 Corinthians 7:1 (KJV)

It is amazing how the clock of life continues to keep ticking during your lifetime, and you can blink your eyes and a new season of life is ushered into your presence. This new and refreshing season of life that you are now experiencing is not only for you, but is also for the people who are closest to you. In the spiritual realm for new believers, this new season of life, after being saved by the amazing grace of our God, is called the process of sanctification.

The process of sanctification is the season of life when you must embrace and celebrate the ideas of total change from that old person that took on the ways of this world to a new person who is now ready to live the good life for God and be free from the bondage of sin. You see when you finally made up your mind to follow God, two forces in the church that day were watching your every move very intently. The two forces that were watching your every movement that day were the forces of good and the forces of evil.

The forces of good were very happy for you that glorious day that you dedicated your life to Jesus Christ. The Bible also states that even the angels in heaven rejoice when a new soul is added to God's kingdom. We now have a living and breathing answer to the many prayers of the saints that were praying for you at your local church, and you have become further proof that the devil is a liar and the power of God will always win in the end.

You now thought that everything would end up just fine, and you could just go home and be left alone, but it won't be that easy. You see, you have just set the stages for the battles for your heart, mind, and possibly your soul, which will now be fought very aggressively by both of these two forces in your life. Yes, you did get saved, but now who are you going to follow?

My dear brothers and sisters, I can tell you with all of the truth in my heart that the forces of evil are not going to just let you walk away from them without a fight. They are going to throw everything at you, including the kitchen sink, for even thinking about leaving them behind.

Do you remember the three major factors that keep you from the grace of God in chapter 3? These three forces: the world's systems, the flesh, and the devil, will now combine their efforts to destroy you or to render your witness totally ineffective to be used for the glory of God.

Now let us look at this word *sanctification* and see what our dictionary tells us about this word.

Sanctification is the act or process of acquiring sanctity, of being made or becoming holy. To sanctify is to set apart for special use or purpose, figuratively "to make holy or sacred."

The process of sanctification is the process of becoming holy and set apart to be used by God, now that you have made Jesus Christ the Lord of your life. This change must now occur in your life to be in the position to be used by God as one of his ambassadors here on this earth. The Bible tells us in 2 Corinthians 5:17 "Therefore if any man be in Christ, he is a new creature: old things are passed away; behold, all things are become new" (KJV).

As you make this transition into becoming a new Christian, people will be watching for this change to occur. This is why during the early stages of your Christian development, a new Christian must be in a true Bible-believing Church and be under the constant preaching of the Word of God.

The people in your church and in the world's systems will now both be expecting immediate change from you. Your response to the lewd jokes and stories at the water cooler at work will be monitored, and these jokes should not be funny anymore after time. People will now purposely start a lewd conversation with you to check your response, and one of the last things you ever want to hear in your life now is that "I thought he or she was a Christian," so beware. The people in the world's systems love to point out a hypocritical Christian, and they will show you no mercy.

During my process of sanctification, I threw my entire collection of pornographic material into the trash and mutilated the entire collection, so that no one else could view this filth ever again. I also went cold turkey with my alcohol addiction with a one-step program called total faith in Jesus Christ.

You will now need to ask this question concerning all of the previous places that you frequented before you got saved by the grace of God. The question is can I bring Jesus Christ into this place with me as my personal guest and be comfortable with him hanging out with me, or would I have to ask Jesus Christ and the Holy Spirit to sit outside in the car and wait until I handle my business? God forbid.

The good thing about being a Christian is that God already knew that this battle for our hearts, minds, and souls would exist, and he knew that mankind could not accomplish salvation by faith alone and continue to remain faithful. The God of the universe would then send mankind a helper or an enabler in the person of the Holy Spirit to help mankind to stay on the right path after being saved by the grace of God.

Now with the Holy Spirit working in us we can now grow in our faith as long as we are provided the constant nourishment of the Word of God in our lives. The Bible tells us in Romans 10:17, "So then faith cometh by hearing, and hearing by the Word of God" (kjv).

Now, let us look at the person of the Holy Spirit. The Holy Spirit is part of the Trinity, which is made up of God the Father, God the Son, and the Holy Spirit.

One of the main jobs of the Holy Spirit is to glorify God, so once you have been saved, you will have an inner force inside of you to help push you to be more Christlike in your behavior, and the Holy Spirit will also help you to increase your faith.

The God of the universe loved mankind so much, that he would send them another tool to help go through the process of change in our lives. The use of prayer can be another effective tool to create change in a believer's life. Just think of prayer as an open line of communication with God's Son Jesus Christ who will hear your prayers, based upon your individual faith and relationship with him.

Please be advised that prayer is a very effective part of your relationship with God, but God will not be mocked. You cannot go out and live like the devil consistently and expect to have a Holy God respond to your prayers.

You can learn more on the power of prayer at your local church, but the power of prayer can give you tremendous power to live the good life as a Christian.

Again, in Christendom, you can make the call on how much spiritual growth that will be working in your life. You can elect to have very little of God's power and the Holy Spirit working in your life or have a lot of God's power and the Holy Spirit working in your life. If you select to have very little of God's power working in your life, then you will become like some Christians just going through the religious experience Sunday after Sunday with no spiritual power to help yourself or to help others. Remember, we discussed this principle in chapter 2.

One of the main problems in the church today, especially in the information age, is that the world's systems and the devil loves to see a new Christian revert back to his or her old ways, and knowing this, the church should do a better job fighting for new souls for God's kingdom. The process of sanctification is a slow process that changes new Christians slowly and not immediately. This entire process must be monitored very closely by pastors, deacons, and church officers.

The process of sanctification is about constant change for a new believer to become holy so that he or she can represent a Holy God. You will not become perfect right away, but you should be striving for perfection during this process. You should start seeing changes in your walk with God, and also changes in how you talk to others in the form of only positive communication.

You will also have to be taught under the authority of your local church because when you are a young Christian, you can be on fire for God, but "zeal without knowledge" is very dangerous. I know some of you mature Christians; can you remember when you were on fire for God?

I can remember when I was a young Christian, I was going to save an old crackhead friend of mine who had destroyed his life smoking crack cocaine. I went over to his house one day (packing heat) armed and extremely dangerous with my Defined King James Bible ready to save him and the entire world that day. I was on fire for the Lord. The funny thing that happened that day was that nobody ended up getting saved, but I ended up losing all of my money due to feeling sorry for my dear old friend. I would then later learn that the worst thing that you could do when dealing with a person addicted to crack cocaine was to give them cash money. The proper response would be for me to take him to a restaurant to get him something to eat or to buy him some medicine.

There are rules of addiction that I was not aware of. My old friend probably used the money that I gave him for food and medicine to go out and buy more crack cocaine. I was now basically prolonging his addiction by giving him the money.

Again, this is why the Apostle Paul teaches us that we must have "zeal based on knowledge," which needs to be taught in your local church.

The Apostle Paul also lays out some things that have to change in you in order to become the new man or woman and start the process of holy living.

> If so be that ye have heard him, and have been taught by him, as the truth is in Jesus: That ye put off concerning the former conversation the old man, which is corrupt according to the deceitful lusts; And be renewed in the spirit of your mind; And that ye put on the new man, which after God is created in righteousness and true holiness. Wherefore putting away lying, speak every man truth with his neighbour: for we are members one of another. Be ye angry, and sin not: let not the sun go down upon your wrath: Neither give place to the devil. Let him that stole steal no more: but rather let him labour, working with his hands the thing which is good, that he may have to give to

him that needeth. Let no corrupt communication proceed out of your mouth, but that which is good to the use of edifying, that it may minister grace unto the hearers. And grieve not the holy Spirit of God, whereby ye are sealed unto the day of redemption. Let all bitterness, and wrath, and anger, and clamour, and evil speaking, be put away from you, with all malice: And be ye kind one to another, tenderhearted, forgiving one another, even as God for Christ's sake hath forgiven you.

Ephesians 4:21–32 (KJV)

Do you see the illustration of the change that must take place?

Old Man	New Man
1. Evil/Worldly	Godly/Righteous
2. Lying	Truth
3. Anger	Joy
4. Stealing	Giving
5. Corrupt Communication	Uplifting Communication

There will be tremendous changes in your life for the better when you start to take on a new Christian lifestyle. The doors of change will now start to fly open for you, based on all of the time and money that you have wasted trying to be happy and have fun outside of an intimate relationship with God. You will have more money available now that you do not spend it all doing the bar scene with people who may or may not even care about you. Your anger levels will now be a nonfactor with your dealings with people in your day to day life. These are just a few examples of possible change, so get ready.

> I beseech you therefore, brethren, by the mercies of God, that ye present your bodies a living sacrifice, holy, acceptable unto God, which is your reasonable service. And be not conformed to this world: but be ye transformed by the renewing of your mind, that ye may prove what is that good, and acceptable, and perfect, will of God.
>
> Romans 12:1–2 (KJV)

The devil, the world's systems, and the flesh want you to conform to what you have been doing all along, which was wasting time, money, and on your way to hell. The new Christian lifestyle now wants your mind to be transformed into the new man or woman who has been changed into a new creature, which is now ready to live an abundant and full life.

I myself was also affected by numerous negative virtues prior to being saved such as viewing pornographic material, alcohol abuse, and hanging out at bars spending all of my money chasing loose women. The new man today is now happily married with a very beautiful wife, clean and sober, and I do not have to worry about possibly catching what they call today as STDs (sexual transmitted diseases). Praise the Lord.

In order to be transformed and to move forward in the things of God, that old man or woman must be left behind in his grave and not be still carried around with you from place to place. Please leave the old corpse in the grave.

Please be advised that when God delivers you from any addictions, please do not look back. Your new Christian lifestyle is now your future, so keep your eyes on the prize, and move forward. Please do not look back at your past, or the devil will make your past life of despair and wasted opportunities your new future once again.

Again, remember the Bible tells us in Matthew 6:24, "No man can serve two masters: for either he will hate the one, and love the other; or else he will hold to the one, and despise the other. Ye cannot serve God and mammon" (KJV).

Remember to keep your eyes of the prize, and never take your eyes off of it. Move forward at all cost.

Chapter Five Summary

A new season for a new believer now saved by the grace of God is called the process of sanctification. This is the season in a believer's life where he or she will be transformed into a new creature by the power of the Word of God and the Holy Spirit.

Sanctification is becoming more like God through the work of the Holy Spirit.

The God of the universe would not leave a new believer without help, but would send the Holy Spirit to help you during this growth process.

The God of the universe would also set up a direct line of communication with all new believers, with his Son Jesus Christ, which is called prayer (twenty-four-hour hotline, no call waiting, better than Facebook).

During this period of intense change, people will be watching for this change to occur, so beware!

The New Man

The Fruits of the Spirit

Love – Joy – Peace – Patience –
Kindness – Goodness –
Faithfulness – Gentleness –
Self-Control

Remember, you cannot serve a Holy God and the devil at the same time. There will have to be a change from your old behavior to serve God.

The new man is possible through faith in God, help from the Holy Spirit, and with a strong determination to move forward with no retreat. Yes, we fall down at times, but we get right back up and keep charging forward because the devil wants your past to become your future.

Yes, there are no perfect Christians in the world today, but I would rather be striving for perfection than being part of the problem in this sick and perverted world that we live in today. We need more Christians who will stand up for Jesus Christ and not be fooled by the devil and the world's systems into thinking that there is any fun in this world outside of a positive relationship with God. Keep moving forward to the things of God. God bless you!

Beware of Evil in This World

The Process of Avoiding Life's Pitfalls

Finally, my brethren, be strong in the Lord, and in the power of his might. Put on the whole armour of God, that ye may be able to stand against the wiles of the devil. For we wrestle not against flesh and blood, but against principalities, against powers, against the rulers of the darkness of this world, against spiritual wickedness in high places. Wherefore take unto you the whole armour of God, that ye may be able to withstand in the evil day, and having done all, to stand.

Ephesians 6:10–13 (kjv)

Today, in this great country of ours, there is a very dark and ominous cloud of evil that is hovering over the United States of America and the entire world. A world-wide spiritual revival is needed today to remove this dark cloud from the face of this planet so that the lights from the heavens can shine on us once again. This great dark cloud that I wish to discuss with you in this chapter is the surge of evil that is in the world today and is encompassing our day to day lives.

The forces of evil in the world today are very well organized and confident that they can win their war against the things of God. These evil forces led by the devil are assaulting our Christian youth movement worldwide by using the Internet and other high tech devices to render young Christians to be ineffective, based on adhering to worldly values and concepts. The Christian youth movement in the world today is critical to our fight because young Christian believers are urgently needed to help constrain the evil in our society for future generations.

The bad news that we face in our society today is that in most cases many mature Christians are losing ground in their fight against evil and are now tolerating the evil in their communities or just giving up the fight.

While on the other hand, evil is spreading quickly throughout most of our communities at breakneck speed, making up its own rules based on greed, creating division, drug abuse, pride, unholy living, poverty, hate, and injustice. We are now also seeing in many cases entire church congregations huddling together in their respective sanctuaries on Sunday mornings and metaphorically closing the windows to the outside world so that they do not have to see the evil that has overtaken their neighborhoods and communities. In some cases, drug dealers and prostitutes are now working right down the street from some of these churches.

I have seen housing projects that are full of despair under siege by the devil and his crew within walking distant from a local church. Where are the Christian soldiers in this country, and who will fight for the Lord?

I can remember not so long ago, my wife and I were invited to an urban inner city church, and we spotted a man crying on his porch across the street from the church that we were attending that day. This man's spirit was broken, the man looked like he was hell bound, and he was living right next door to a church. God forbid!

I asked the young man why wasn't he a part of God's program at this local church, and his answer to my question shocked me. His answer to my question was that no one had ever asked him to come to church before our conversation that day. Why are we allowing the devil and the world's systems to win strategic battles for the minds of our men and women without a fight?

In the world today, we are seeing people who used to fear God, but are now running wild in most communities, strung out on dope with no hope for their lives and robbing churches. This new practice of robbing churches was totally unheard of in the past. This is something that is entirely new in our communities because no one back in the day would get up enough nerve to rob a church during the night-time hours. Today, we are seeing crooks robbing churches at night consistently on the evening news, and during the day on Sunday mornings, the congregations are robbing God by not paying their tithes and offerings.

In most churches in this country today, we are seeing no altar calls, no baptism, and nobody being brought into God's kingdom. The world today needs a true revival soon with the church of God leading the way worldwide, or Jesus Christ must come back soon and take his church out of the world because the future of Christendom is looking very dim. Christianity is currently trying to fight a war with only a faithful few soldiers on the battlefield. God only needs a remnant!

My question to all of the Christians is: where is the moral majority in this country and who is standing up for the truth of God's Word in the workplace and at the ballot box? The moral majority of this country is mostly Christian, but we continue in this country to lose ground on such hot button issues as gay marriage, abortion, gun control, and the filth in the media.

In our society today, gay talk show hostesses (who are women, but are dressing up to look like men) are now confusing the youth in America into thinking that this alternative lifestyle is the way God created mankind to be. Not only are Christians watching this filth, but these same gay talk show hostesses on television today have in the past been awarded Emmy awards for this sick perverse practice of deceiving the youth in this country. Now don't get me wrong because I love gay people and I know God loves us all. I am a living and breathing example that God is able to change anyone, just like he changed me, but we all must want to go through the change process. The bad media situation does not stop with the problem of alternative lifestyles being portrayed in the television industry in this country alone.

Today, you cannot turn on your television set without seeing numerous commercials with only a little of the actual programs, which are mostly old reruns of the same old movies going from one network to another.

The language in these movies continues to be filthy by even worldly standards, with the men and women in these movies pushing the envelope exhibiting sexual lust-filled behavior, with women's breasts fully exposed for all to see, and our children are watching this filth.

The evening news is also totally biased today, working along both the Democratic and Republican Party lines with news networks like Fixed (Fox) News blatantly lying to get their points across. I have now had to set aside some time for a personal Bible study in the evening to avoid these huge pitfalls of wasting my time during the evening hours. Another big problem in this country is that a lot of Christians are spending their precious time trying to be authorities on the ways of this world and not enough time studying things that pertain to God's kingdom. I have sat in Bible College classes and was shocked to hear some of the political views of these Christian New Age thinkers. I am now seeing Bible students in this country building their biblical foundations on worldly philosophies and not on the Word of God.

Today, schools are not teaching their students the fundamental truth that God is still in control of this world that we live in and that we may be losing the fight these days, but we know the final outcome of the war which is written in our Bible. We win!

The goal for this chapter is to get all Christians mad at the way things are going these days and to force former Christian soldiers that are AWOL back unto the battlefield to start taking the fight to the enemy prior to the return of Jesus Christ. Today, we have far too many Christians standing and watching while souls are being lost on the battlefield of life. A great part of the teaching of Jesus Christ in parabolic form was to have saved believers work hard for the things of God right up to his return and not taking on the ways of the world or living like the devil until he comes back for his church. My problem is that how can we continue to fight the world's systems when most Christians think like the world and are being pressed into their mold. Again, even though we know we win in the final battle against evil, we still need to try to save every soul on this planet from the eternal separation from a Holy God and from a very bad place called hell.

In this chapter, we will quickly examine four pitfalls that are plaguing Christendom and are causing soldiers to stop fighting the good fight for God in these last days.

The Christian life is about avoiding pitfalls, but we are all overcome by some of these issues in our walk with God at one time or another. The good thing about being a Christian is that when we fall down, we can get right back up and serve the God of this universe again. We only need to repent and change from our wicked ways, and God will always forgive us because he loves us so much. Sometimes, identifying these pitfalls can help us all to stay clear from evil and also give us the clarity that evil does exist in this world, so beware.

Beware of the Devil

> Be sober, be vigilant; because your adversary the devil, as a roaring lion, walketh about, seeking whom he may devour: Whom resist stedfast in the faith, knowing that the same afflictions are accomplished in your brethren that are in the world.
>
> 1 Peter 5:8–9 (KJV)

The entire nations of this world today face a clear and present danger that is a master of disguise, who goes by many aliases, and is a pathological liar. This clear and present danger in the world today is the evil initiated by a created being that goes by the names of satan, lucifer, or sometimes just called the devil. This created being is armed and extremely dangerous and has with him one-third of the host of heaven helping him to create mayhem and destruction wherever he goes here on earth. If you were to see the devil, which most of you have, please do not try to apprehend him. You are only to resist his advances standing firm in your faith because he has already been judged and his sentence will be carried out at a later date in history. Christians especially need to beware of satan and to never give into his advances because it will only mean the start of sinful behavior and possible separation from God in the end. One of the biggest reasons today why we are not getting fresh troops unto the battlefield of life to advance God's kingdom is due to the massive attacks by satan's legions on Christendom. Now let us look into who satan really is.

Again, one of the greatest enemies that face people who believe in Jesus Christ goes by many names as stated above and listed below.

1. Lucifer – Which means Light Bearer. This does not mean that satan is the true light like God!

2. Satan – The great opposer or adversary. His job is to stop you from Godly purpose.

3. Devil – Diabolos, a slanderer, an accuser. He is the enemy of man's spiritual interest.

These are only a few names that the devil has been called throughout his history. Remember back in chapter 1 that satan's greatest trick played on mankind is to make mankind think that he only exist in the minds of believers and in the Holy Scriptures. This statement is far from the truth. The devil is a real created being who was one of God's greatest creations before his wisdom was corrupted.

The Bible describes satan in the Book of Ezekiel:

> Son of man, take up a lamentation upon the king of Tyrus, and say unto him, Thus saith the Lord GOD; Thou sealest up the sum, full of wisdom, and perfect in beauty. Thou hast been in Eden the garden of God; every precious stone was thy covering, the sardius, topaz, and the diamond, the beryl, the onyx, and the jasper, the sapphire, the emerald, and the carbuncle, and gold: the workmanship of thy tabrets and of thy pipes was prepared in thee in the day that thou wast created. Thou art the anointed cherub that covereth; and I have set thee so: thou wast upon the holy moun-

tain of God; thou hast walked up and down in the midst of the stones of fire. Thou wast perfect in thy ways from the day that thou wast created, till iniquity was found in thee.

By the multitude of thy merchandise they have filled the midst of thee with violence, and thou hast sinned: therefore I will cast thee as profane out of the mountain of God: and I will destroy thee, O covering cherub, from the midst of the stones of fire.

Thine heart was lifted up because of thy beauty, thou hast corrupted thy wisdom by reason of thy brightness: I will cast thee to the ground, I will lay thee before kings, that they may behold thee. Thou hast defiled thy sanctuaries by the multitude of thine iniquities, by the iniquity of thy traffick; therefore will I bring forth a fire from the midst of thee, it shall devour thee, and I will bring thee to ashes upon the earth in the sight of all them that behold thee. All they that know thee among the people shall be astonished at thee: thou shalt be a terror, and never shalt thou be any more.

Ezekiel 28:12–19 (KJV)

Most Bible scholars believe satan possessed the king of Tyrus in the above Scripture. This gives us our first ability of satan. Satan can take on the forms of men and animals. Remember satan in the garden of Eden?

Satan was God's greatest creation. He started off perfect in all his ways before his rebellion. He was beautiful and adorned with all sorts of precious stones. Satan is also a musical creature (who loves choirs) and was the anointed cherub that covererth the very throne of God. It sounds like satan was very high in the hierarchy in the heavenly realm before he was cast down to the earth to war against the things of God.

The question in my mind is: Why is satan so mad at God? Why does satan fight so ferociously when he knows that he cannot win? You see, when satan was created, he was created just like you or me with free will, and satan rebelled against God. He put his will ahead of God and thought he had a chance to be God. Satan's greatest crime is that he wanted to be God.

In Isaiah 14:12–15, the devil set his agenda against God's authority:

> How art thou fallen from heaven, O Lucifer, son of the morning! how art thou cut down to the ground, which didst weaken the nations! For thou hast said in thine heart, I will ascend into heaven, I will exalt my throne above the stars of God: I will sit also upon the mount of the congregation, in the sides of the north: I will ascend above the heights of the clouds; I will be like the most High. Yet thou shalt be brought down to hell, to the sides of the pit.
>
> Isaiah 14:12–15 (KJV)

Now that we know satan's time is running out, let us look at defeating satan based on the Word of God:

1. The first tactic to defeat satan: Satan is the father of all lies and the accuser of all believers. Christians must be people of truth in most cases and tell the truth at all times, or we will put ourselves

in league with the devil's schemes and methodologies. Satan's people will always accuse you first, and then expose you, so do not get caught lying (tell the truth).

2. The second tactic to defeat satan: Satan is not all knowing and cannot be in all places at all times, like God (omniscience/omnipresence).

   Satan counters this weakness with the ability of his hierarchy of demons who provide him information. Today many non-suspecting, good-natured Christians in most cases are telling satan's crew of fallen demons how to destroy us and inflicting friendly fire on our troops. Christians need to stop volunteering information to satan's people over the telephone, Facebook, tweets, texts, and in personal meetings.

3. The third tactic to defeat satan: The use of the doctrine of separationalism. Do not try to be friends with the forces of evil because it will never work. The Lord is going to be the only one you can count on in this world today. Real friends in this world are far and few. Please only fellowship with Godly people, and leave the devil's people alone. Continue to try to save lost souls, but beware.

Now I beseech you, brethren, mark them which cause divisions and offences contrary to the doctrine which ye have learned; and avoid them.

Romans 16:17 (KJV)

And have no fellowship with the unfruitful works of darkness, but rather reprove them.

Ephesians 5:11 (KJV)

Beloved, believe not every spirit, but try the spirits whether they are of God: because many false prophets are gone out into the world.

1 John 4:1 (KJV)

4. The fourth tactic to defeat satan: To resist the devil's evil plans for your life. Fight him standing firm in your faith in God. Remember in the spiritual realm, the Bible tells us in Hebrews 11:6, "But without faith it is impossible to please him" (KJV).

In James 4:7, "Submit yourselves therefore to God. Resist the devil, and he will flee from you" (KJV). He is going to keep coming but keep resisting.

5. The fifth tactic to defeat satan: Good old-fashioned prayer. A good soldier will win most of his battles on his knees. Tell your Holy Father on him, and God will send some angels to help you.

Again, there are many other tricks that satan is playing on believers today, but they're the same old tricks such as lying, trying to make you doubt God's Word, and twisting the Word of God.

You young Christians will need more training in your respective local churches, and you mature believers get back into the war. Please report back to duty today!

Beware of the devil and his evil team of fallen demons.

Beware of the World's Systems

> Love not the world, neither the things that are
> in the world. If any man love the world, the love
> of the Father is not in him. For all that is in the
> world, the lust of the flesh, and the lust of the
> eyes, and the pride of life, is not of the Father, but
> is of the world. And the world passeth away, and
> the lust thereof: but he that doeth the will of God
> abideth for ever.
>
> 1 John 2:15–17 (KJV)

Today, we are experiencing significant signs of an old
unholy alliance of joint cooperation that is being forged
anew, and this old alliance is now stronger than ever. This
evil alliance has been in existence in this world since
the beginning of mankind, but is now bonding together
tightly to wreak havoc on our world communities. The
unholy alliance that I wish to discuss in this chapter is
formed between the world's systems and the devil. The
world's systems are unlike the devil, whose methodologies are somewhat standard in their applications such as
lying, twisting the Word of God, accusing believers, and
exploiting negative situations. On one hand, the devil
is still up to his same old tricks that he has perfected
through the ages, but the world's systems on the other
hand has now gone high tech to destroy believers quickly
with all types of new technology and also new tactics.

Now let us define what are the world's systems?

The world's systems are not defined by the physical
world that we live in, which God created from nothing

when he created the heavens and the earth. The world's systems are the world that is here on this earth that believers share with people who do not have a relationship with God. You see people in the world today without a relationship with God operate under another set of rules and principles that do not exist in the spiritual realm. These rules and principles, which people who do not have God working in their lives, are diametrically different than the rules and principles that believers adhere to and firmly believe in, based on the Word of God. The world's systems is also interlinked with the devil and his hierarchy of demons with two goals in mind, which is to stop Christians from achieving Godly purpose for their lives here on earth and to send as many people as they can to a place called hell for eternity.

Characteristics of the world's systems are listed below:

1. The world's systems rules are built on certain ideas such as greed, the negative use of ambition, and financial rewards to achieve personal objectives. The battle cry of the world's systems is that greed is good, and forget about the other guy because I need to get what is mine.

2. The world's systems lives for today and does not look at things eternal. Most of the music that is being pumped through the airways these days to the youth in this country addresses only living for tonight because tomorrow cannot be guaranteed. This type of thinking by the world's systems is killing the youth of this country and is a recipe for disaster in many cases. Bullying is also part of the world's systems self-centered thinking.

3. The world's systems promotes a permissive sexual lifestyle unlike God's creation of marriage between a man and a woman. In the world's systems, any immoral act is accepted, based on putting no belief in moral values, and disregarding the absolute truth in the teaching of God's Word.

4. The world's systems makes up their own rules to maximize their own pleasure without Godly virtues. The world's systems slogan is to do anything until you're satisfied, and forget about the consequences that tomorrow will bring.

5. The world's systems will try to pervert God's Word based on false philosophies by these so-called New Age thinkers. The world's systems has its own theology that is draped in universalism and multiple paths to eternal life. (More on new Age Thinkers later.)

6. The world's systems are very high on plastic surgery (breast enhancements, tummy tucks, face-lifts, butt lifts, and botox injections) to fix up the outer you, but does nothing to make you a better person with Godly virtues.

In our main text, the Apostle John writes concerning the three major components that the world's systems use to take your focus off God. These are the lust of flesh, the lust of the eye, and the pride of life.

Now let us look at the three components of the world's systems:

The lust of the flesh is the sensual gratification in the world today, which is running wild between worldly men and women who are seeking sexual gratification to fill a void that God has reserved for him only in their hearts. You see, when God created mankind, he created an area in the hearts of mankind for his love only. If you do not find his love based on the Word of God, you will fall prey to all types of worldly temptations that will just keep you craving for more and more of any immoral sexual act or drug to fill this void. After a while, without the love of God in your heart, true love will not become achievable without true repentance. (This is why the rich and famous have so many problems.)

Beware of the lust of the flesh.

The lust of the eyes is the temptation from worldly gratifications, such as on the Internet, cheap magazines, gaudy dress, or a sexual attraction for someone other than your spouse. We are now in the information age where everything is at your beck and call on the end of a touch screen or at the click of a mouse. You can now have pornographic smut piped into your home without a trip to the red-light district of your hometown. In our society today, pornography is a multi-billion dollar industry over the Internet with revenues rising every year. Not only is the world's systems enjoying this easy access to filth at the push of a button, but so are many Christians also struggling with these problems. Pornography is a major pitfall that we all need to avoid by not plugging into the Internet or going to these illicit Web sites.

In our society today, we are also seeing most women in this country accentuating what they consider as their positive assets on the exterior of their bodies. If a woman has nice legs, then she will wear tight miniskirts, and if a woman has full breasts, she will then wear low-cut blouses to reveal her breasts for all to see.

I can remember back in the 1970s if you wanted to see loose women, you had to go to the red-light district in downtown Springfield, Massachusetts. The women, who frequented what we called the "hoe stroll" downtown, had their breasts fully exposed, wore tight miniskirts, and had high heel platform shoes with their feet exposed. Today, you can fast forward to 2013 and you can find this same style of gaudy dress in most office buildings, on your job, and (God forbid) in some churches.

What used to be so cheap has now gone mainstream. Now even the so-called nice girls want to look like cheap hookers. My wife and I went to funeral a year ago and we saw numerous women with their breasts exposed at a funeral; the people at the funeral that day were dressed up like they were going out to a nightclub. This has become a huge problem in the African-American communities where death is now being devalued these days. Whatever happened to showing some respect for the dead, yourself, and for others?
Beware of the lust of the eye.

The pride of life is hunting after honors, titles, and wanting to have all this stuff here on earth that will keep you broke (keeping up with the Joneses or the Kardashians). I have fallen prey to this same old trick of the devil and the world's systems. Remember, that the devil will bless you with stuff and also bestow titles, but it is never worth the cost. Only what you do for God will last in this world and into eternity. We are now seeing some great men of God who no longer want to be called pastors or reverends any more, but now they want to be called apostles. After the devil fooled me into accepting a title, my favorite title now is a *man of God,* and I would not trade this title for all the money in the world. *Beware of the pride of life.*

In the world today, believers face many enemies in their daily walk with God. On the other hand, the people in the world's systems walk around fat, dumb, and happy until they find out that having it their way will never work. Only some worldly people will turn to the only true help for their lives, which is a relationship with Jesus Christ. The other people in the world's systems who do not seek Jesus Christ for help will continue to fight the teachings of Jesus Christ all the way to hell, which will someday be their final resting place. We need to work hard at reaching unsaved people. Jesus Christ is our best example of reaching the lost. He saved a man from hell while bearing the tremendous pain hanging on the cross. Jesus Christ never stopped trying to save lost souls!

On the other hand, rather than being out saving souls, today we have millions of Christians plugged into the Internet wasting their time surfing the web instead of studying their Bibles. The world's systems are now using technology to control people and keep them connected to what I call the control grid. This control grid keeps the world's systems and most believers connected through laptops, headphones, dumb phones, tweets, texts, and the devil's new favorite tool, Facebook.

Today, both Christians and non-Christians are obsessed with plugging into the grid for the latest nonvalue communication and gossip between each other that they are not finding any time to pursue Godly virtues. We are also seeing most businesses are now tapping into the power of the grid and requiring their workers to connect their lives to their companies by laptop or dumb phones so that they will be at their beck and call any time of the day or night. We are now becoming a Godless society with the main emphasis on being connected to the grid and to each other by e-mail, text messages, and even tweets, which is choking out the Word of God from this Christian nation of ours.

During the recession in 2009 and also in the slow recovery that we face today in America, businesses are now holding on to their cash and not hiring American workers (greed).

This hiring issue has affected every industry in this country and most American families. Most American companies just continue to squeeze their workforce to do more with less while the companies enjoy record profits and huge cash reserves.

Again in corporate America, we are now finding out that your boss did not do you any favors letting you bring your laptop computer home and work from the confines of your home. Now that he has you connected to the office mainframe (the grid), you will soon be subconsciously using your laptop at home for work projects and neglecting more important things like a relationship with a Holy God. The world's systems have now gone high tech with the use of trickery!

I have heard numerous people in my old office telling me that they would go into their e-mail on Sunday and clear out all of their messages, so that Monday morning would not be so stressful.

Business in this country is also linked up with the devil and the world's systems and has now even crossed the line and is scheduling work on Sundays in most cases. God forbid this practice!

We are now seeing people in the world's systems and most Christians going to work on Sundays rather than attending church services these days. You see the devil and the world's systems do not mind paying double time for working on Sundays if your main focus is on them and not on God. The devil considers this to be money well spent when he can entice a Christian to skip church to earn overtime consistently.

Satan is now basically laughing at Christians, who trust in him more than they trust in God. The irony of this practice by ignorant Christians is that anyone who will trust the devil will never enjoy what he has to offers. Be it money or some sort of pleasure, if you do not do things the Lord's way, he will put holes in your pockets and you will stay broke, and all this additional overtime will never really help you. Only the things that you do for God will give you lasting fulfillment; when will people finally realize this simple fact?

Beware of the world's systems!

Beware of Sin

For the wages of sin is death; but the gift of God
is eternal life through Jesus Christ our Lord.

Romans 6:23 (KJV)

The word *sin* began its origin in a garden that was called
Eden, in the Bible book of Genesis in the Old Testament.

This Garden of Eden was a perfect environment and it
met all of the needs of the garden's inhabitants, who were
named Adam and Eve. One would think that mankind
would be happy living in this perfect environment, but
that was not the case. Mankind has been wallowing in
sin since the tragic day that the word *sin* was conceived.

The Bible tells us in Romans 5:12, "Wherefore, as by
one man sin entered into the world, and death by sin; and
so death passed upon all men, for that all have sinned"
(KJV).

We see in the two Scriptures above that sin has always
been associated with death. In the world in which we
live, excessive sin will definitely physically kill you, but
in the spiritual realm sin will separate you from a loving
God, causing spiritual death also. You see, God loves us
all, the criminals, gay people, and everyone else in this
world which we live in, but there is one thing that God
truly hates and that is sinful behavior.

What is sin? I will give you a few definitions. Sin is
an act that violates the moral laws of God. Sin is also
committed by putting your will against the will of God
based on his Word, which is the worst kind of sin called
rebellion. Sin is the hatred of what is good and the love

of what is evil. In short, sin is anything that goes against God's Word.

The problem that we face in Christendom concerning sin is that every one of us on this planet is a sinner, both Christians and non-Christians. The Bible tells us in Romans 3:23, "For all have sinned, and come short of the glory of God" (KJV). We all have a sin nature from birth, which is inherent in us. Have you ever watched a young child's behavior? They want what they want now, and they will do whatever they have to do to get what they want. It is now up to their loving parents to limit their selfish behavior and do what is good for the family unit. We all know that children are self-centered, and this trait can follow their behavior into adult life if not corrected. This is the same type of principle that applies to Christians who are not perfect like little children, but we are all trying to change by the grace of God. The Christian lifestyle should be to avoid sin in your life at all cost and to never be overcome by sinful behavior. Our goal is to be a holy people!

Please take note again that Christians are not perfect, and sometimes, we will mess up. All human beings mess up in their walk with God sometimes. The good thing concerning Christianity is that the loving God that we serve will forgive you if you seriously repent, turn from your evil ways, and change your sinful behavior.

We all need to beware of sin in our lives because sin is destroying the institution of marriage in this country, among other Godly institutions.

Today, we are seeing a tremendous rise of infidelity and immorality in our society because of more rapid forms of communication these days.

Most people who are caught in infidelity today are using cell phones and text messages to communicate with someone other than their spouse. Today, one of the number one causes of couples breaking up in this country is due to text messages left on a cell phone by a friend with benefits or someone other than their significant other. Wow!

A famous poet has equated sin to a spider's web: because once you get caught in the web of sin it is hard to get out. Sir Walter Scott tells us, "Oh what a tangled web we weave, when first we practice to deceive."

Let us now look at three characteristics of sin that are listed below.

1. Sin will take you further than you wanted to go.

    Since time began on this earth, people have attempted to sin and tried to hide this sin from a loving God. Can you remember the story of Adam and Eve in the Garden of Eden? When will people learn that you cannot hide from God because he is in all places at all times. People today drive to other cities to have affairs, take drugs, and to do all sorts of immoral behavior, but in the end, they always end up getting caught. When will people learn that anytime you partake in sinful behavior, the devil and his people will always expose you especially if you are a Christian? God also sees your sinful behavior, and he is not pleased with you. Beware of where sinful behavior takes you!

2.   Sin will cost you more than you wanted to spend.

How many people in the world today wish that they had all of the money they have spent on sinful behavior? In this country alone, we spend billions of dollars on illegal drugs and immoral sexual behavior to feed our sin nature. I feel for the poor children who sometimes do not have anything to eat because their mother or father is strung out on dope or is at some gambling casino under the perception that they are having so much fun in life. These kids are the real victims of the price paid for sinful behavior. No one wins when sin is flourishing in your life. Beware of the cost of sin in your life because this cost is always too high and it will lead to your destruction!

3.   Sin will always keep you longer than you wanted to stay.

The hands of a clock never turn in the sin process. If you look carefully, you will never see a clock or the light of day in a gambling casino or in a crack house because the house wants you to stay until all of your money is gone.

All sinful activity will only be available for as long as your money lasts, and then you will have to leave and come back with more money if you want to resume this sinful behavior.

You see clocks and windows are absent in a sinful environment to make you lose track of time and reality, but the true reality of the situation is that you are always going to lose and the house

will always win! Beware of sinful behavior, which
has no time limits.

The Bible is very clear about sin, even though we serve
a loving, caring, and forgiving God that Christians should
never continuously be entrapped or overcome by sinful
behavior. The world, on the other hand, loves sin until it is
too late. You can just watch the television show *Celebrity
Rehab*, which is predicated on celebrity dope addicts who
have now gone broke and have no hope in their lives. The
devil and the world's systems are now all finished with
these people, and nobody wants to hire them. I watch
this show to help me to study addiction, which is one of
my new paths in life. These people need to find God in
their life and not more television work if they want to
change their lives. They need to get into a one-step program called faith in Jesus Christ. I am finding out that
drug abuse is trying to plug a void in a person's life that
only a relationship with God can fill.

Young and mature Christians, please stop all sinful behavior. The Bible tells us in Ephesians 5:14–16,
"Wherefore he saith, Awake thou that sleepest, and
arise from the dead, and Christ shall give thee light. See
then that ye walk circumspectly, not as fools, but as wise,
Redeeming the time, because the days are evil" (KJV).
Beware of sin in your life.

Listed above are only a few pitfalls that you will
encounter. Please get further training at your local church
on all of these biblical concepts.

My dear brothers and sisters, confess your sins to God
now and never look back.

The Bible tells us in 1 John 1:9, "If we confess our sins, he is faithful and just to forgive us our sins, and to cleanse us from all unrighteousness" (KJV).
Beware of the pitfalls of sin in your life.

God bless.

Beware of Unrighteousness

THE CLYDE PRINCIPLE

Now therefore thus saith the LORD of hosts;
Consider your ways. Ye have sown much, and bring
in little; ye eat, but ye have not enough; ye drink,
but ye are not filled with drink; ye clothe you, but
there is none warm; and he that earneth wages earneth wages to put it into a bag with holes.

Haggai 1:5–6 (KJV)

In the world today, one of the biggest problems that we encounter in this Christian nation of ours is that we have far too many self-professing Christians who are walking away from the loving arms of God and conforming to this present world while the devil and the world's systems are triumphantly cheering them on. The Bible is very clear about this subject. The closer we come to the Lord's second coming that many false prophets would come on the scene, and many people would not want to hear Godly Bible teaching anymore. Christians need to get back into the churches of this country and stand up for Godly principles in the workplace before it's too late.

During the spring of 2011, I opted to take an early retirement to rid myself from a company that wanted me to keep my entire focus on their products, and what other little time that I had left over just maybe I could scrape up enough time to worship the God of this universe. The plan that this company had for my life did not work, and God took me out my comfort zone and started his rebuilding process.

You see, when God rebuilds a man, it will never be in a penthouse apartment on Times Square or in a Beverly Hills estate, but he will sometimes rebuild you as a garbage collector or a cleaning person doing some sort of menial labor to humble you. You Bible scholars need to figure out this teaching.

It was at a lowly hotel job doing manual labor after my early retirement from a lucrative position in the aerospace industry where I got my best lessons in human nature and humility. I also got a chance to sharpen my skills in spiritual warfare, based on constant attacks from the demonic presence at the hotel, coupled with the many New Age thinkers whispering in the ears of the poor workers at the hotel who did not have God working in their lives.

At this hotel, which I affectionately called the Belly of the Beast, I met a brother named Clyde who would teach me firsthand what the definition of a closet Christian was, along with the many other people working at this hotel professing to know God. I could now see that the devil in low levels of society in this country along with the world's systems are now trying to claim victory in the war against the things of God by using covetous tactics, rage, filthy speech, and a profound love for money. It is ironic how money affected these people working at this hotel so adversely.

The average hotel worker was only getting paid minimum wage at best, but most of the workers at this hotel would rat out their momma to get more overtime or to impress the bosses who would keep this vicious cycle going full circle.

At the hotel, I was constantly getting accused by the workers for real petty things, and I was being cussed out constantly by numerous women who had mouths so filthy, it would make you cringe. These women at the hotel would use cuss words that would make a seasoned sailor blush with envy, and they could drop the F-bomb impressively only to themselves in every one of their sentences.

The good news about my situation was that I could now visualize and see firsthand that the devil hates to see a man of God come into his domain and try to change things. I was only successful by working harder than anyone in this hotel and just killing these stiff-neck people with love and kindness.

Soon, to my amazement, the attacks stopped and the people around me started showing each other a little kindness, which began to be contagious when they interacted with me. The concepts of being kind to people who may even hate you showed me what the Gospel of Jesus Christ was all based upon, which was to love God first and to love the people around you even if they are trying to stab you in the back or cuss you out for no apparent reason. I learned that when you respond to evil with love and are courteous to people, evil cannot flourish in this environment. I also learned that we can defeat evil using strong Christian principles and truly change the behavior of the people around you in most cases.

It was at this hotel I would learn yet another valuable lesson from Clyde, who was a self-professing Christian who was scheduled for work every Sunday and would not even darken the doors of the house of the Lord to worship or to praise him. My man Clyde would talk about the Lord only when I would mention it to him first, but if Clyde had been in a court of law, they could not have never convicted poor Clyde of being a Christian, due to lack of evidence. But Clyde knew all of the buzz words and talked about the days when he used to go to church.

Now I will never judge another man's salvation, and I truly believe that Clyde probably did get saved at one time in his life, but there are millions of people like Clyde who know the Lord, but are totally conformed to the world's systems, which has now become their new god. I would curiously watch Clyde on his cell phone every day talking to family members and friends like he was someone very important working on a janitor's salary. I would have thought that all this money Clyde was spending on his cell phone, which had all of the bells and whistles, would be better used in his savings account at a local bank. But poor Clyde was plugged into the world's systems and was being blinded by the devil.

My man Clyde's main hustle at this hotel was that he had access to the trash from the hotel rooms, and he was making a killing confiscating the beer and food that was left in the rooms on the weekend shifts, Sundays in particular.

The guests at the hotel would leave these items in the rooms, and when they checked out, Clyde would bring these items back to his poor neighborhood in which he lived and pretend to be some type of Robin Hood character.

At the hotel, Clyde had a huge reputation for taking just about anything out of the rooms, even open food, but soon, he would finally get caught in his web of sin. (Everyone gets caught!)

You see, Clyde's biggest mistake was that he took some food out of a room of a person who was still a guest at the hotel, and he got caught by an eyewitness account. This problem of taking things from the hotel rooms had now become a major problem for him because this was not the first time Clyde had been in trouble for taking things out of the hotel rooms and was eventually let go from the hotel.

I was shocked when the devil's man at the hotel told me that he was standing outside of the office door when they brought poor Clyde into the office to discuss the food that was missing from the room, and Clyde's whole defense was that God knows that he did not take the food out of the room.

The devil's man at the hotel kept telling me over and over again how Clyde kept invoking the name of Jesus Christ and saying God knows he did not take the food.

The devil's man also forcibly interjected in our conversation that something must have been very wrong with Clyde because he had worked with Clyde for a very long time and he had never heard anything about God come out of Clyde's mouth before. There were also other people at the hotel who were standing outside of the door, listening and laughing at poor Clyde while the managers were questioning him, and they were also dumbfounded by his statements concerning God, based on Clyde having absolutely no evidence of being a Christian to anyone other than me. The bad news about this entire situation was that they fired poor Clyde, and I tried to contact him on that cell phone with all of the bells and whistles to encourage him, but his phone was disconnected.

Soon, God opened up my eyes and revealed to me that one of the major problems that we face in Christendom today is that we have far too many Clyde's not providing a positive witness in American society today. These are the areas where the Church and Christians must stand up and be an example for God's kingdom.

> Then shall they call upon me, but I will not answer; they shall seek me early, but they shall not find me: For that they hated knowledge, and did not choose the fear of the LORD: They would none of my counsel: they despised all my reproof. Therefore shall they eat of the fruit of their own way, and be filled with their own devices. For the turning away of the simple shall slay them, and the prosperity of fools shall destroy them. But whoso hearkeneth unto me shall dwell safely, and shall be quiet from fear of evil.
>
> Proverbs 1:28–33 (KJV)

This story concerning poor Clyde is again the story of countless other Christians in this country who think that God is not watching and that they cannot change the world around them. This is not true and the devil is a liar! The truth of the matter is, through the power of the Word of God, you can be victorious in all endeavors.

Christians in the evil world that we live in today cannot afford to wait until times get tough to call on the Lord, but honor and worship him when times are good, so his peace will surround you during the rough times.

Today, we are seeing an alarming number of Christians in this country living in worse conditions than the people in the world's systems or the people currently on the devil's payroll, due to not following God's plan for their life.

All Christians are commanded by the Word of God to stand up for God's kingdom today and be a walking, talking advertisement that will show God's love to the evil world in which we live.

The Bible tells us in Matthew 5:14–16:

> Ye are the light of the world. A city that is set on an hill cannot be hid. Neither do men light a candle, and put it under a bushel, but on a candlestick; and it giveth light unto all that are in the house. Let your light so shine before men, that they may see your good works, and glorify your Father which is in heaven.
>
> Matthew 5:14–16 (KJV)

This country is predominately a Christian nation based on every poll taken in this country of ours, so why are we losing so many battles in the courts and in our workplaces?

The answer to this question is that the devil and his people are holding their ground and standing up for their rights in this country to stop the things of God, but on the other hand, Christians instead of standing up for God, they are retreating to their closets and only crying out to God in private when things finally start to unravel. The Lord is putting holes in the pockets of all Christians who are not standing up for the Gospel of Jesus Christ in these tough times in which we live. I urge all closet

Christians to come out, come out, wherever you are, and fight for Jesus Christ now before he comes back and then it will be too late. Remember, you are on the winning side of this battle, please make a difference in your surroundings, and in the people's lives around you. Don't be like Clyde!

> Not every one that saith unto me, Lord, Lord, shall enter into the kingdom of heaven; but he that doeth the will of my Father which is in heaven. Many will say to me in that day, Lord, Lord, have we not prophesied in thy name? and in thy name have cast out devils? and in thy name done many wonderful works? And then will I profess unto them, I never knew you: depart from me, ye that work iniquity.

Matthew 7:21–23

Beware of becoming a closet Christian.

Saints, we are living in our last days and times. If you fit any of the examples in this chapter, it is time to change immediately and get things right with God before it is too late!

Last Days and Times

And, behold, I come quickly; and my reward is
with me, to give every man according as his work
shall be. I am Alpha and Omega, the beginning
and the end, the first and the last. Blessed are they
that do his commandments, that they may have
right to the tree of life, and may enter in through
the gates into the city.

Revelation 22:12–14 (KJV)

In the world today, the Church of Jesus Christ is still that
great big beacon of light that continues to shine on saved
believers, based on being of divine origin. The Word of
God also still has the power to save lost souls just as it did
two thousand years ago during the first coming of Jesus
Christ. We are now seeing God's master plan unfold in
the world today, that in the end times many would stop
following the Holy God of this universe and would start
following the god of this present world which is the devil.

It is common knowledge, even among most nonbelievers, that Jesus Christ came to this earth the first time
based on the Holy Scriptures. My question is, if Jesus
Christ came once into this world based on the Scriptures,
why wouldn't he come back again based on the Holy

Scriptures? I will not pretend to have any sort of secret knowledge to somehow know the day, the month, or the year of his return, but our Lord and Savior Jesus Christ is coming back soon. It is now our job as Christians to be working right up to his return trying to reach lost souls to tell them about a better life here on earth that can blossom all of the way into eternity.

In the world today, we are seeing many of the Bible prophesies being revealed right before our very eyes. The world is seeing an increased number of earthquakes constantly with higher magnitudes than past earthquakes as foretold in our Holy Bible. We are also observing every night on the evening news conflicts going on all over the globe with wars being fought on most continents in the world today. At the time of the writing of this book, the United States of America is presently fighting in one war in the Middle East and funding numerous other wars in many other nations. The world today is seeing famine, drought, and pestilence everywhere in the world, even in rich nations like ours.

The accomplished Bible student will always use history as a barometer to see the future, but his best weapon to see the past, the present, and the future direction of this world is by studying his Holy Bible.

We are now seeing that the United States of America today has the very same problems as did the late great Roman Empire. The Roman Empire was destroyed primarily by three things, which was their military power was overextended, moral decay, and debt problems. Today, we see the United States government and most governments in Europe are all on shaky ground financially due to massive debt problems.

In most worldwide political systems, the team concept of helping people and compromising for the good of the people means nothing anymore. The worldwide political system has now become all about the power of individual groups who have formed their own sense of reality, and it is now "my way" or no way at all. In the world today, these individual groups are so divided in their own political views that they are now turning the truth into a bunch of lies to reflect their own mostly self-centered agendas. (No one is willing to compromise their position) Remember chapter 1!

The moral fiber in the United States of America has also deteriorated so badly in this country that our leaders are being plastered across newspapers and on the evening news on a daily basis. I am talking about church leaders and secular leadership, such as United States senators and congressmen. Don't get me wrong, I love the United States of America dearly, but I thank God that my hope does not lie in the leadership structure of this nation. My hope lies in the only person who can permanently fix this mess, which is the God of the universe Jesus Christ in his second coming.

Millions of people in this country today are now putting all their hope in Barack Obama, who is a good man, but he cannot stop biblical prophecy. We see millions of other people worldwide are placing their hope in the new pope, but he is way off on his theology with no true way to help anyone anymore. Lastly, millions of people are now putting their hope in Oprah, Dr. Phil, Dr. Oz, and all these so called reality show characters that come on the boob tube daily. Unfortunately, this world keeps deteriorating at a record pace and these reality show personalities just keep on getting richer.

My dear brothers and sisters, as things in this country continue to go from bad to worse, there is a bright light coming at the end of the dark tunnel for us Christians, and it is called the second coming of Jesus Christ. This is a hope that all Christians can count on, and while we wait, we can live a good life here on earth without the evil that is all around us.

Today, Christians everywhere are patiently waiting for the return of Jesus Christ with true anticipation without the fear of physical death, but with the true reality of life after death based on the hope given to us by the Holy Scriptures. You see, the world's systems and the devil have no plans for you after you die. People, even by the world's standards, want to go to heaven, but nobody in the world's systems wants to die first. The Gospel of Jesus Christ has taken away the fear of death from true believers and has planted the seeds of hope in things eternal.

Yes, we Christians want to live a full and long life just like anyone else, but a true Christian understands that we are only passing through this life and our bodies are truly groaning to be with God in the heavens. On the other hand, the unsaved live their lives without any eternal security and just make up their own rules for their existence, which is only short term at best and lacking true Godly wisdom.

My final appeal in this chapter will be based on many good reasons to dedicate your life to a loving God, but the security that the Gospel of Jesus Christ would bring you should be a major factor in your decision to become a born-again Christian. I truly believe with all my heart if Jesus Christ was to return today, it would not be a minute too soon. My only hope is that he will find me working hard, trying to do some good in this world that is getting increasingly more evil every day. Today, I walk confidently in my salvation, knowing to be absent of this fleshly body I will be with my heavenly Father for eternity.

The Word of God states in Hebrews 2:14–15:

> Forasmuch then as the children are partakers of flesh and blood, he also himself likewise took part of the same; that through death he might destroy him that had the power of death, that is, the devil; And deliver them who through fear of death were all their lifetime subject to bondage.
>
> Hebrews 2:14–15 (KJV)

You see, the devil wants the people in the world to be in constant fear of things to come just like he is because he knows that a place called hell will be his eternal home along with his fallen demons and everyone else here on this earth that he can persuade to come with him.

The freedom of the Gospel of Jesus Christ should be a very positive reason to dedicate your life to God, along with many other reasons that come to mind, such as clean and sober living. There are many other reasons for becoming a Christian that have been spelled out in detail in this book from my perspective, but you too can see that you can have the abundant life here on earth with a relationship with God.

In this last chapter, we are going to look into four reasons unsaved believers need to give their lives over to Jesus Christ before it is too late. Time is getting short, and God is coming back soon! Remember, this decision must be made before you die, and this decision is not negotiable. Everyone on the face of this earth will have to choose someday who they will follow whether it is good, or evil.

A Leaderless Society Awaiting a New Leader!

> And then shall that Wicked be revealed, whom the Lord shall consume with the spirit of his mouth, and shall destroy with the brightness of his coming: Even him, whose coming is after the working of Satan with all power and signs and lying wonders, And with all deceivableness of unrighteousness in them that perish; because they received not the love of the truth, that they might be saved.
>
> 2 Thessalonians 2:8–10 (KJV)

The world today is facing a new phenomenon of leaderless groups that are now taking over small shopping malls or entire nations of people in the blink of an eye. We are now witnessing in the world today that the power of the grid (social media) can assemble a flash mob at your business in minutes for good or evil purposes by just sending out tweets to people passing by.

Today, entire governments are changing hands in such places as Libya, and our government does not even know if the leaders of these rebellions are either friends or foes, due to no one strong leader standing up front and leading the charge in these rebellious groups.

In the United States of America, the Occupy Wall Street movement was one of those leaderless groups who challenged authorities in this country and created a national movement with no one person standing at the helm of leadership.

We have another leaderless group of people in this country called the Tea Party, who have created mayhem in our political system here in the United States. It is another great example of a group of people who wants to create change by not compromising and creating their own set of values.

The world's political systems today are now on the brink of failure and ready to fall due to non-compromising political leaders and the rise of gutter religious systems throughout the world.

In the Bible book of Daniel, the weakest part of the statue in King Nebuchadnezzar's dream was in the feet, which were made of iron and clay. Most theologians surmise that if a political system is poorly run by uncompromising people, this system will not stand long before it will crumble.

Today, we are finding out that good, strong leadership has become a thing of the past. We are now basically living in a leaderless society that is lacking good old-fashioned moral judgment. If the *Titanic* was sinking today, you would see a bunch of big, strong men safe inside the confines of all the life boats alive and well, and the poor women and children that were on that tragic boat would now reside at the bottom of the sea. You see, when you take Christian principles out of the schools and colleges of this country and replace these principles with worldly standards, true leadership cannot flourish.

It will not be long before the God of the universe is going to let the devil and his team of fallen demons appoint their own leader so that mankind again can be happy and have a great charismatic leader, just as God let the children of Israel have an evil king named Saul.

The world today is being prepared for a new leader who will lead the world astray, and he will be far more evil than any of his predecessors and he will have the power to counterfeit many signs and wonders for his adoring public. This leader will be very different from the leaders we see today and will be out front leading the charge for all to see and will be a very eloquent speaker for all to hear.

In the 1930s, the nation of Germany was racked with unemployment and dissention with their government leaders, similar to what we are seeing in the United States today. The German government had many freedoms, which gave all of the people a chance at a good life in pre-Nazi Germany, but the German people wanted a leader who would preach what their itching ears wanted to hear.

You see, Adolf Hitler used the democratic system with all of its freedoms to rise to power, and when he achieved total power, Adolf Hitler turned Nazi Germany into a dictatorship with no freedom at all. Adolf Hitler would then go on to form one of the most evil governments in the history of this world and the people of Germany followed him attentively to the very end.

Once again, this world is searching desperately for a great and powerful leader, and the forces of evil will soon gladly heed the clarion call by the unsaved world. The entire nations of the world today are now getting ripe and ready for the picking to do what mankind has always done throughout the history of the world, which is to choose evil over good.

The rise of an evil leader. Coming soon!

The Rise of Misses Mousey

> Notwithstanding I have a few things against thee, because thou sufferest that woman Jezebel, which calleth herself a prophetess, to teach and to seduce my servants to commit fornication, and to eat things sacrificed unto idols. And I gave her space to repent of her fornication; and she repented not.
>
> Revelation 2:20–21 (KJV)

The Spirit of Jezebel is alive and well in the world today.

Toward the end of the twentieth century, this country was going through a fundamental change in the business climate of this nation that would change the way Americans do business for generations to come. A new cry erupted loudly from American businesses in this country to outsource as many American-made goods and services to low-cost foreign businesses in Western Europe, Pakistan, India, and China. This calculated move by American businesses was to cut the high cost of paying American workers and to increase the profit margins on American goods and services.

Greed was now the new way of doing business in the United States of America!

The internal structure of the Old Boy's network would now also change as these jobs were being sent overseas, and there would be no need for all of these top heavy corporations full of men running these businesses. Soon, most businesses started giving out lay-off slips and separation packages to get these older, high-paid managers out the door with some type of dignity. The businesses in this country loved the lay-offs and the separation packages due to the enormous cost savings involved, but found out that the lay-offs and separation packages were stripping away all of the male managers who had a vast knowledge of their businesses.

The rise of Misses Mousey got its start as these older, high-paid male managers were being shown the door in this country, right up until this very day. Besides, these new women managers would also provide another cost savings to these companies for every older man that she replaced because her salary would be substantially less than her male counterpart. (Misses Mousey was now born and on the move.)

Today, the current workforce in this country has a very high number of good, competent, and loving Christian and non-Christian women working at predominately all levels of American society, and I have been truly blessed by working with many of these good women.

Now who is Misses Mousey?

Misses Mousey represents a very small group of career women who are predominately white women, but she can also be a non-white woman (African-Americans and Latino-Americans).

Misses Mousey is somewhat educated and is now ready to take on all of the challenges that the world's systems may bring her. The problem with Misses Mousey is that she wants to take on all of these challenges, under the power of her will only, and not under the power of Jesus Christ and the Holy Spirit.

Miss Mousey differs from the old feministic views of another era where many feminists would state: I don't need a man to be successful, or I will probably have kids after my career gets off the ground. Today, Miss Mousey wants it all now: she wants a nice husband that she can control, she wants the big house in a suburban setting, she wants children, and lastly, she wants the family structure that God has ordained. Again, the problem with Miss Mousey is that she wants all of these things without a relationship with God because her schedule is far too busy.

Most Americans are saying while reading this article what is wrong with wanting to have it all?

This statement has a very simple answer. The problem with wanting the good life without God has its consequences, and it may not be manifested in you, but these consequences may come into play in the people that you love. Also, the good life can never be achieved without a relationship with God.

After I retired in 2011, I sought some temporary work to help support my many ministries. I could not find a temporary agency that was not staffed without an office full of women trying to discuss with me things about aerospace manufacturing that they did not understand or quite truthfully knew anything about.

These women staffing agencies would send me on temporary assignments to American companies who would be also staffed with women working 24/7 that were all stressed out, moody, and with a common problem of having huge issues at home with their children or with their husbands who were now playing second fiddle to their careers. At this one job that I worked at, they had a woman purchasing manager who did not really understand purchasing at all, but her greatest asset was that she could communicate in the language of the parent company, and she was also well connected in this company. This woman's entire management team was all women with only one man in a somewhat managerial role, and none of these women as I saw it had any relationship with God outwardly. All of these women were all too busy trying to get the latest gossip and trying to show their tough side instead of showing the side that God created women to be, which is kind, loving, nurturing, and encouraging.

Again, what is wrong with a woman achieving success and promoting their own gender?

Being a student of history, I can remember when there were no black American or women managers in the workforce at all, and the civil rights movement for racial equality in the workplace was lock step with the women's rights movement in this country. Both of these great movements worked hard to get equality into the

American workforce. Many people died to help black Americans and women get equal rights.

Today, Misses Mousey has now moved up to the top of the food chain and she is doing the same thing that the Old Boys' network has done in the past, but now she is actively promoting what I call the new girl's network.

The new girl's network is excluding minority women and competent men for management positions now that they are in charge of running these companies on an operational level only.

During the late twentieth century, the crack cocaine epidemic went through most urban neighborhoods like a hurricane, leaving death and destruction everywhere within its path. The states, federal, and local governments were powerless to stop the carnage, and nobody really cared anyway because this epidemic was somewhat confined to poor urban neighborhoods. Today, you cannot turn on the news without seeing crime and drugs in what the news media call sleepy little towns where these types of things never happened before. Drugs, crime, and gun violence is now running rampant in these upscale communities where the kids are robbing their own neighbors blind.

Remember that my own success lies in seeing my dear mother's love for God and not the love she had for her job as a means of success. My mother was a pioneer at her job and a dynamo at the church who loved the Lord, and she knew where her bread was buttered. (Jobs come and go, but the Lord is here forever.)

Today, Misses Mousey is engaging with what I call *pacification parenting* by trying to have it all in life without God, which is destroying the family unit as defined in the Bible. We are now finding out that in most upscale neighborhoods, a whole generation of children who are not trained to make any sort of moral judgments, but are given the latest electronic gadgetry to pacify them and not educate them in the way to live the good life based on the Scriptures.

The Bible tells us in Proverbs 22:6, "Train up a child in the way he should go: and when he is old, he will not depart from it" (KJV).

In this chapter, please do not get me wrong, I am not hating on the success of women, but I am hating on these Godless career woman's spiritual failure that is unleashing a lost generation of spoiled, self-centered, Godless children into this world with no moral values. I am not jealous of Misses Mousey either because my mother had it all: she had God in her life and a loving family, and her career was a very distant fourth or maybe fifth on her list of priorities.

Remember, a God-fearing mother in society today can bring tremendous hope in any child's life, but a mother who does not educate her children in the things of God nor does she fear God is setting the stages for disaster in everyone's life around her.

Misses Mousey please help to stop this new generation of evil!

The Rise of the False Prophets in This World

Beware of false prophets, which come to you in sheep's clothing, but inwardly they are ravening wolves. Ye shall know them by their fruits.

Matthew 7:15–16 (KJV)

Today, lurking in the world, there are many voices whispering into the ears of believers for good and for evil purposes. Mankind should not feel that this is something new because there is nothing new that mankind can conceive or invent in their minds that has not happened in past history or has not been foretold that would happen in the future. Today, based on the Scriptures, the world is seeing many false prophets that are spreading hate and negative thoughts to an adoring public professing to be someone who is wise.

The Bible is crystal clear when it warns believers that in the last days that many false prophets would appear on the scene and would deceive many people. Today, in the media age of 24/7 communication, we are seeing a rise of what I call Babel, or confusion, that is trying to teach mankind another way to attain eternal security without a strong belief in Jesus Christ, which is not the truth based on the Holy Scriptures. Today, these false prophets are hard to spot because they are pretending to be Christians when they communicate with Christians, but they can also adapt to non-Christian thinking and fit into nonbelievers' beliefs of multiple paths to heaven without God.

You see, these New Age thinkers as I call them, simply try to be all things to all people and blend in with anyone. The most important thing that Christians need to know is that these people work for satan and want to control you based on corrupting your thinking. These New Age thinkers are armed and extremely dangerous to Christians because they do not truly believe in God and do not want you to believe in God either.

The Apostle Paul describes these people in 2 Timothy 3:1–5:

> This know also, that in the last days perilous times shall come. For men shall be lovers of their own selves, covetous, boasters, proud, blasphemers, disobedient to parents, unthankful, unholy, Without natural affection, trucebreakers, false accusers, incontinent, fierce, despisers of those that are good, Traitors, heady, high minded, lovers of pleasures more than lovers of God; Having a form of godliness, but denying the power thereof: from such turn away.
>
> 2 Timothy 3:1–5 (KJV)

The Apostle Paul describes these people and also gives believers the solution of what to do when a believer should encounter a New Age thinker or false prophet. My dear brothers and sisters, when you run into these people leave them alone. (Try to help get them on track, but beware.)

Again, these New Age thinkers or false prophets are nothing new to the world today. New Age thinkers have been part of satan's plan since the beginning of time.

In the Bible book of Genesis, these evil men at the Tower of Babel knew God had great creative power first-hand, but they did not have faith in God. These evil men in early civilization would soon try to bypass God to get to heaven under their own will and build a tower that reached the heavens. This plan did not work!

Today, New Age thinkers are still trying to build that Tower of Babel based on a religious system of thinking to get to the heavens by creating a sense of reality in their minds that is not biblical. The new forms of communication, such as the Internet and twenty-four-hour news in the information age has increased the amount of Godless chatter that people are being exposed to these days to 24/7 exposure. Today, we have political talk show hosts and radio personalities who claim to be Christians, but all you hear come out of their mouths is negative conversation. These media people are making huge sums of money to tear down a political party or an individual person, just because he or she does not share their vision on a particular hot button issue and do or say absolutely nothing that truly glorifies God. These New Age thinkers are now everywhere trying to be authorities on the world, based on the thinking of the world, and infecting anyone who will listen to this garbage.

Now let us look into what is a New Age thinker.

1. A New Age thinker is a person who has a "form of godliness, but denying the power thereof," which means a New Age thinker will act like a Christian, but truly he or she does not believe in God. These people have more faith in worldly concepts than they have faith in God.

2. A New Age thinker is a person who believes in multiple paths to salvation and that a good God will never send a good person like me to a burning hell. These ideas on eternal security are not only dangerous, but they are not biblical.

3. A New Age thinker does not believe that going to church has any benefit in gaining any type of spiritual knowledge or spiritual well-being for people. These people will always tell you that they have read the Bible or me and God talk all of the time!

4. A New Age thinker is well versed with all worldly political concepts due to spending an enormous amount of time watching news-related garbage and not taking the time to study the Word of God in most cases.

    Most New Age thinkers take a negative command of a political system along a party line and are part of the problem and not part of the solution.

    A New Age thinker bombards his or her life with negative radio shows or news stations, and they think that they are receiving some sort of secret knowledge from these millionaire wind bags preaching hate (Russ Limbaugh, Sean Hannity, Al Sharpton, conspiracy literature, Fixed News/MSNBC).

5. A New Age thinker has a non-compromising attitude, and he or she will always have to be on the right side of any argument and will never admit to being wrong (not a truly happy person).

New Age thinking is becoming very fashionable these days, due to mankind's thirst for knowledge outside of a relationship with God. The mainstream media is capitalizing on this thirst for non-value news that creates division and points out a worldly lifestyle.

Does anyone ever look out into their communities these days on their way to church and see most of the people are cutting their grass, washing their cars, or just milling around in the yard on Sunday mornings? Again, does anyone ever compare notes over the weekends with the office staff on how they spent the weekend? Today, many people in the world are authorities on worldly political ideology with little to no knowledge of God's Word and do not even darken the doors of a church on Sunday morning.

After I retired from the aerospace industry, I had the chance to work in many facets of American society and attend secular schools and also Bible institutions.

Today, Americans are too busy to attend church regularly anymore (God forbid). The millions of people who are working in this country today are doing twice the amount of work than they used to do with the constant threat hanging over their heads of still being laid off. This business climate puts people under so much pressure that they try to impress their bosses and bring home their laptops to send out e-mails over the weekend, but they are still given even more work to do the following week. When will people learn that impressing the boss will never work, he or she will only find more work for you to do? We need to impress Jesus Christ!

The Bible tells us that a "little leaven will leventh the entire loaf," and millions of people today are being infected by these New Age thinkers. These New Age thinkers have shown up at many of my temporary job assignments and have even tried to hijack my own thoughts with their negative philosophies, but I can spot these people a mile away now! Do you know how the treasury of the United States trains its agents on how to spot counterfeit currency? The answer to this question is that they familiarize their agents with the real thing. This is the same way Christians need to spot negative communication in the world today by constantly listening and reading the truth of God's Word. True believers need to digest only positive communication 24/7.

Christians today should become seekers in this great laboratory that we call life here on this earth and to search the Scriptures and the world to see how we measure up against God's Word. Please stay far away from New Age thinkers (false prophets) in these last and evil days; you will know them by the fruit that they bear. Study the Word of God and you will be able to spot these people quickly and not fall prey to their evil attacks on your mind.

The Bible tells us in 2 Corinthians 11:12–15:

> But what I do, that I will do, that I may cut off occasion from them which desire occasion; that wherein they glory, they may be found even as we. For such are false apostles, deceitful workers, transforming themselves into the apostles of Christ. And no marvel; for Satan himself is transformed into an angel of light. Therefore it is

no great thing if his ministers also be transformed as the ministers of righteousness; whose end shall be according to their works.

2 Corinthians 11:12–15 (KJV)

Stay away from New Age thinkers or False Prophets.

The Rise of a New Generation of Evil Is Being Born

Train up a child in the way he should go: and when he is old, he will not depart from it.

Proverbs 22:6 (KJV)

In the world today, a new generation of children is growing up in this country that will tip the scales of balance in the spiritual war of good versus evil. This new generation of children today will be far different than past generations of children growing up here on this earth, due to the fact that this new generation will in most cases have little to no knowledge of Jesus Christ or the Holy Scriptures. This new unholy generation of children will not have the ability to make any type of moral judgments and will have grown up entirely in the information age under the supervision of every sort of negative communication tool that world's systems has at its disposal.

Today in the information age, we are seeing that this younger generation is mainly focused on the latest electronic devices to waste hours upon hours of time being connected to the grid or to some other high tech devices. I myself have observed a little girl in our family playing with a little handheld electronic device for hours, sitting at the kitchen table all by herself, and she was just fascinated sitting there without parental supervision. Today, many parents are using these electronic devices to babysit their children rather than spending time to educate children in proper moral behavior.

The role models for all of the children growing up in society today are only focused on fame and fortune with little to no mention of God in their interviews or any type of moral uplifting message. We are seeing every new generation getting less and less concerned about doing good in this world and more adapted to self-centered thinking and evil thoughts. Even Hollywood is now attacking this new generation of young people with films that sensationalize the dark and evil side of life (vampires/demons). This love for the dark side of life is setting the stages for a dark future where any evil thoughts are acceptable.

As the tables continue to turn and the paradigm continues to shift, the United States of America may not be a Christian nation anymore in the near future. This new evil generation, coupled with the rise of Islam in this country and other worldwide cults, which are invading the thoughts of our American students at many of this country's junior colleges and universities where New Age thinking, is surging at an all-time high. The God of the Bible is not pleased!

Has anyone walked through the shopping malls or into the classrooms of the colleges and universities of this country lately? Yes, we have become a more diverse society, but the people in America no longer look like you anymore and definitely do not think like you.

In the near future, the next generation of Christians will not have the same freedoms in this country or in the world, due to being persecuted, tormented, and laughed at in this new society formed by a new generation of children, if the Lord does not tarry and come back soon.

If you are employed at certain jobs in this country in the near future and they find out that you are one of them people (Christian), you may find yourself getting fired or not in the raise pool that year. If you are in a local college setting your views on life and morality, will be ridiculed, and even your professors will encourage you against this perverse Christian thinking. Lastly, the media will belong to satan in the last days and times and he will be plastering the air waves of the world with his ungodly theology 24/7, brainwashing everyone around you.

The encouragement that I can give this new generation is that our God is still on the throne and he is faithful, and he will always make a way for his people. The Lord throughout history has only needed a remnant of people to project his will and his power on mankind. The rise of this new generation that does not know God in the end times is going to make it very hard for Christians in the future, but remember, you are still on the winning side of this battle.

Now that we have looked at some biblical events that are unfolding in our society today, Christians do not need to now just give up and sell all of our possessions and wait for the Lord to come back. Christians need to live the good life here on earth and be a walking and talking billboard for Jesus Christ. The Bible is very clear that a true Christian needs to be working for the kingdom of

God right up to the very day of the return of our Lord and Savior Jesus Christ. Christians in the household of faith need to be pushing hard to save every lost soul possible from a very bad place called hell, and as he appears in the skies, he will be able to tell you face-to-face, "Well done, my faithful servant. Well done!"

Hearing these words from our Lord and Savior Jesus Christ is the goal of every Christian, so let's roll up our sleeves and get to work today!

> Wherefore he saith, Awake thou that sleepest, and arise from the dead, and Christ shall give thee light. See then that ye walk circumspectly, not as fools, but as wise, Redeeming the time, because the days are evil.
>
> Ephesians 5:14–16 (KJV)

> Jesus saith unto him, "I am the way, the truth, and the life: no man cometh unto the Father, but by me."
>
> John 14:6 (KJV)

As we now come to the end of this book, we have had many goals set in our journey together like finding Jesus Christ in your life, finding the truth in the world today, being a part of God's institution the local church, and the existence of evil in the world. These were some lofty goals, but I believe that we covered all of these topics in-depth in the pages of this book.

With God's help, the first goal of this book is to assist you with finding a meaningful relationship with Jesus Christ and that he has been brought into your life. To my many readers who have already been saved by his amazing grace my hope is that his Spirit has been rekindled in you and that you will embrace his institution the local church for comfort and spiritual well-being in these last and evil days. You may not be perfect, but as long as you keep the Lord your rock of salvation, there is nothing to fear, but fear itself.

The second goal of this book is that I hope that you will find the truth in your life. The world today desperately needs the truth due to everything being subjective in the eyes of mankind. You see, mankind has been searching for the truth since the times of the Roman Empire when Pontius Pilate asked Jesus Christ the question, "What is truth?" due to not understanding what the truth was. In the world today, Christians need to understand and live their lives based on an absolute truth, which is the Word of God. You see, without an absolute truth in your life, you will only create your own truth to live by, based on your own sense of reality or the reality of the people that live around you.

Furthermore, I pray that another goal of this book has been accomplished, and you will now understand that we live in a world today that is getting exceedingly more evil than past generations in this country, and that evil truly does exists in the world today. My hope is that you would see that doing some good for your fellow man and living based on the absolute truths in God's Word can counteract the evil all around you, and you can live the good life here on earth.

When a false prophet or a New Age thinker tells a Christian in these last days and times that there is no reason to go to church, we must remember that the Lord's church provides believers with order, spiritual balance, and hope in a hopeless world. We also must remember that we cannot love God without loving his institution, which is the local church, and if anyone tells you anything different, they lie and they do not tell the truth.

Lastly, if this book has helped to lead anyone to salvation, stay faithful and continue to enjoy the many benefits of the Gospel of Jesus Christ. Because the ways of this world are only causing people today to kill, steal, and live very unhappy lives as they are being played out on your television screen, the Internet, and in your newspapers on a daily basis. If the Lord has delivered you from a life of darkness, please keep moving toward his marvelous light and seeking a positive relationship with our Lord and Savior Jesus Christ before it is too late. Remember the characteristics of a person seeking God from chapter 1?

My Story Update

Yea, and all that will live godly in Christ Jesus shall suffer persecution.

2 Timothy 3:12 (KJV)

Today, as I write the final pages of this book, my beautiful wife is fighting a serious medical condition, and I am also fighting some serious health issues. I am now semi-retired and working to supplement my ministry as a contractor in the aerospace industry dealing with all kinds of negative personalities that do not know God, but I continue to look up to God every day who is faithful. I hope that this does not disappoint any of my readers that I do not have a good worldly report that I am now living in a big house, driving a Bentley, and living larger by worldly standards, which is not the case. During this time of my life, my friends and most family members have all deserted both me and my wife. They have written us both off for our tremendous faith in God, but again, the Lord has been faithful and is standing with us.

If you get anything out of this book, it is that we all need to find God in our lives and never look back. A relationship with him is the key to true happiness, and he is the only one who can provide you with joy when all is lost. Your friends and some family will come and go, but God will always be with you because he is truly faithful. The world wants you to be happy by worldly standards, but the joy of the Lord is given only to believers who can remain joyous in bad times and in good times. Today, I am the richest man in the world, but maybe not from the world's perspective, but based on my knowledge of him.

My brothers and sisters, continue to fight for good in this world that we are just passing through while we are in anticipation of our blessed hope that we have in Jesus Christ. The key to the Gospel of Jesus Christ is love, and it will sustain you, and you can have the good life here on this earth before his triumphant return. My wife and I have never been closer, and we wake up every day with a song in our heart, thanking God for this happiness that surpasses any imagination that man could ever dream up or comprehend.

Sorry no big car. Sorry no big house. Sorry no big money.

But we serve a big God, who can provide true love and happiness into your life.

The defense rests its appeal.

Let us hear the conclusion of the whole matter: Fear God, and keep his commandments: for this is the whole duty of man.

For God shall bring every work into judgment, with every secret thing, whether it be good, or whether it be evil.

Ecclesiastes 12:13–14 (KJV)